To Know You And Not Love You Is Abnormal

Ernest Solivan

To Know You And Not Love You Is Abnormal

To Know You And Not Love You Is Abnormal

ISBN: 978-0-6151-9402-8

Artwork by
Susanne Valla

Printed in the United States of
America by Lulu Publishing

Back cover photo of
Susan Solivan, age 39
by Nanette Fenton

To Know You And Not Love You Is Abnormal

In Loving Memory Of Susan Solivan
1946 —2014

"In my loneliness, when I'm all by myself and I need your caress, I just think of you and the thought of you holding me near makes my loneliness soon disappear. Though you're far away, I have only to close my eyes and you are back to stay, I just close my eyes and the sadness that missing you brings soon is gone and this heart of mine sings."

Antonio Carlos Jobim

Introduction

To Know You And Not Love You Is Abnormal

At the very beginning of our relationship in the mid 1980s, my wife Susan and I wrote notes to each other almost daily. Our mornings were structured so that both of us would be in the kitchen alone for ten minutes or so at different times. This book is a compilation of the notes I had written to Susan.

You must first understand that my wife Susan is the loveliest and most delightful human being I have ever met. The scope and depth of my love for her literally astounded me.

I was and still am amazed at my capacity to love which Susan so adroitly extricated from the depths of my soul. I used every metaphor and simile I could beg, borrow and steal to mirror this experiential bliss back to its source. At no point in my life can I ever remember my imagination being as taxed as it was during this period.

I had the honor and privilege of being Susan's husband for 29 years which my Soul will cherish for Eternity, and although Susan is no longer with us, much to the detriment of everyone who knew her and the rest of the occupants of Planet Earth, I am certain that whomever she comes in contact with in the Spirit World will be, as I was, totally delighted with her presence. And, I know that the God of her understanding as well as all the other inhabitants will stand in line to lovingly welcome her with open arms.

The toll of this profound loss for me is incalculable, and it is with infinite sadness that I console myself knowing that Susan is safe and at peace wherever her Spirit went. I longingly look forward with joy and glee to once again reuniting with the love of my life. I am certain that if there is no Heaven they will surely create one for Susan.

It is my wish that every human being on this planet experience what I have and am still experiencing with Susan. The euphoria, I believe, stems from the realization that you can unconditionally love someone, and your value is such that you warrant a reciprocity of that love.

For those of you who are reading this book who have never experienced it, think of this way. Remember the best compliment you ever received, then multiply it by 1,000,000,000,000. I sincerely entreat the reader to treasure and savor every nanosecond spent with your Beloved.

The first time I listened to Puccini's Nessun Dorma sung by Luciano Pavarotti after Susan's passing I wept, and at that moment I realized they were not tears of sadness, but tears of joy. The joy I experienced spending 29 years with the most delightful and loving woman I had ever met.

I lovingly and respectfully dedicate this book to the woman whom, because of my love for her, I have objectified as the most loved woman who ever lived. Susan Solivan.

Monday, March 4th

I wanted to see my love for you. So, I took
my heart and held it to the light.
I saw a breathtaking sunset,
a baby feeding at mother's
breast and your
lovely smile.

I Love You

Thursday, March 7th

Oh soulmate of centuries past, it is wonderful to see you once again. Your warmth is penetrating, your embrace is soothing, and your beauty is un-questionable. Just as I remembered you.

I Love You

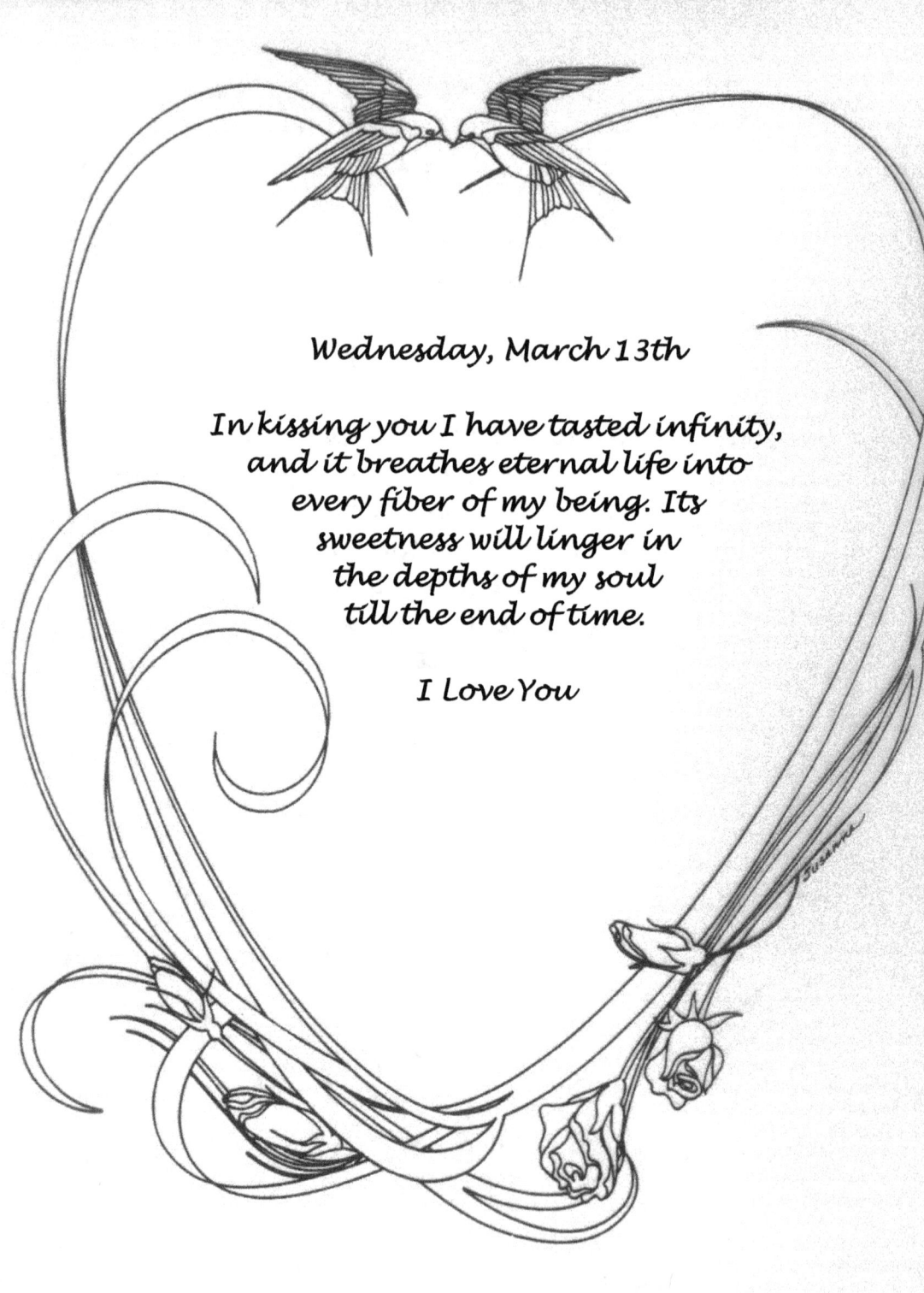

Wednesday, March 13th

In kissing you I have tasted infinity,
and it breathes eternal life into
every fiber of my being. Its
sweetness will linger in
the depths of my soul
till the end of time.

I Love You

Friday, March 22nd

T.G.I.F.Y. Thank God I Found You. I have searched for you since the beginning of time. Where were you?

I Love You

Monday, April 8th

Your breath is like Universal honey.
With every exhale, the nectar of its
essence fills the atmosphere,
and anyone lucky enough
to breathe it in is forever
changed.

I Love You

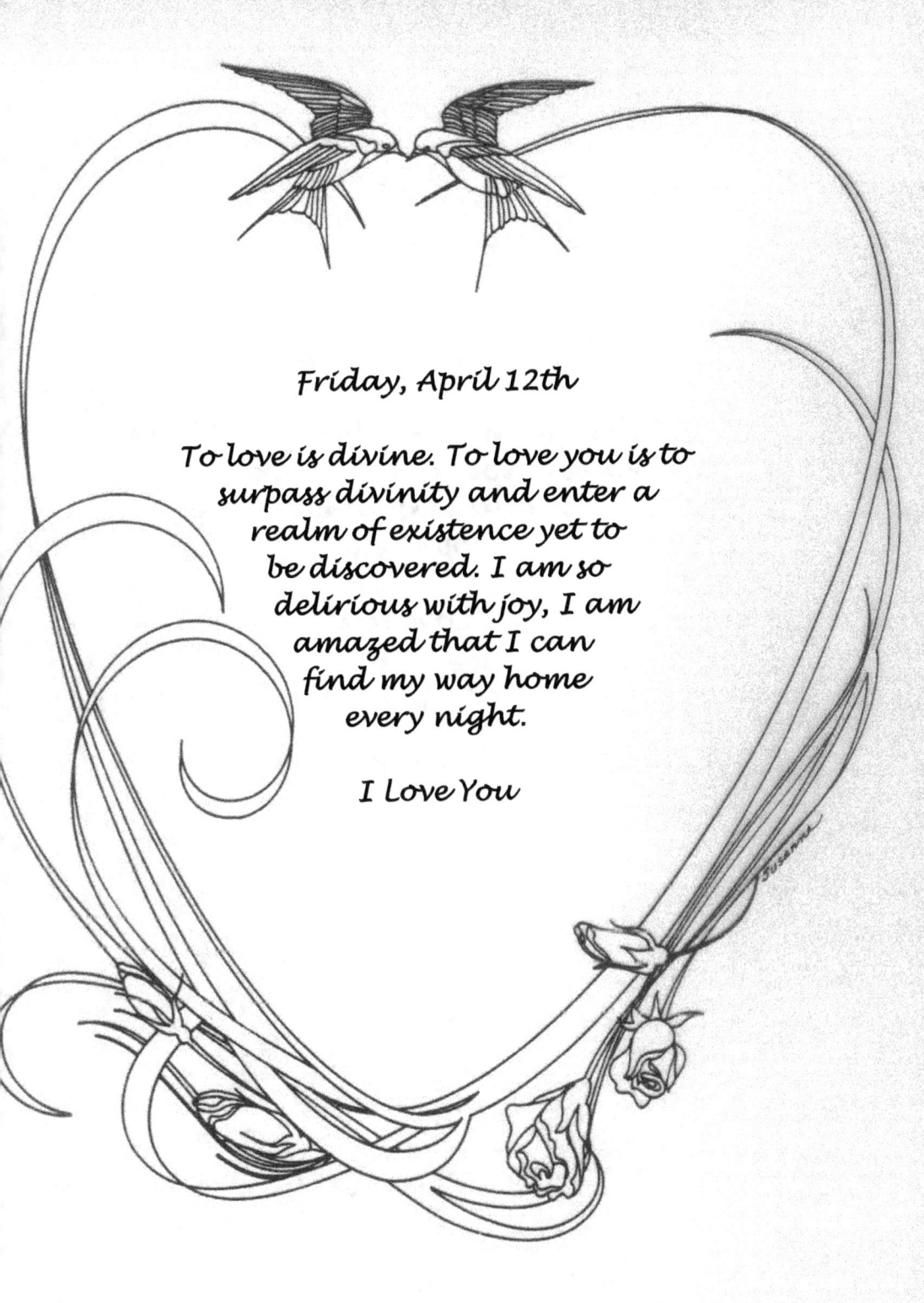

Friday, April 12th

To love is divine. To love you is to
surpass divinity and enter a
realm of existence yet to
be discovered. I am so
delirious with joy, I am
amazed that I can
find my way home
every night.

I Love You

Tuesday, April 16th

If there were no God, they would have
to invent you, and I am certain
Voltaire would have
approved.

I Love You

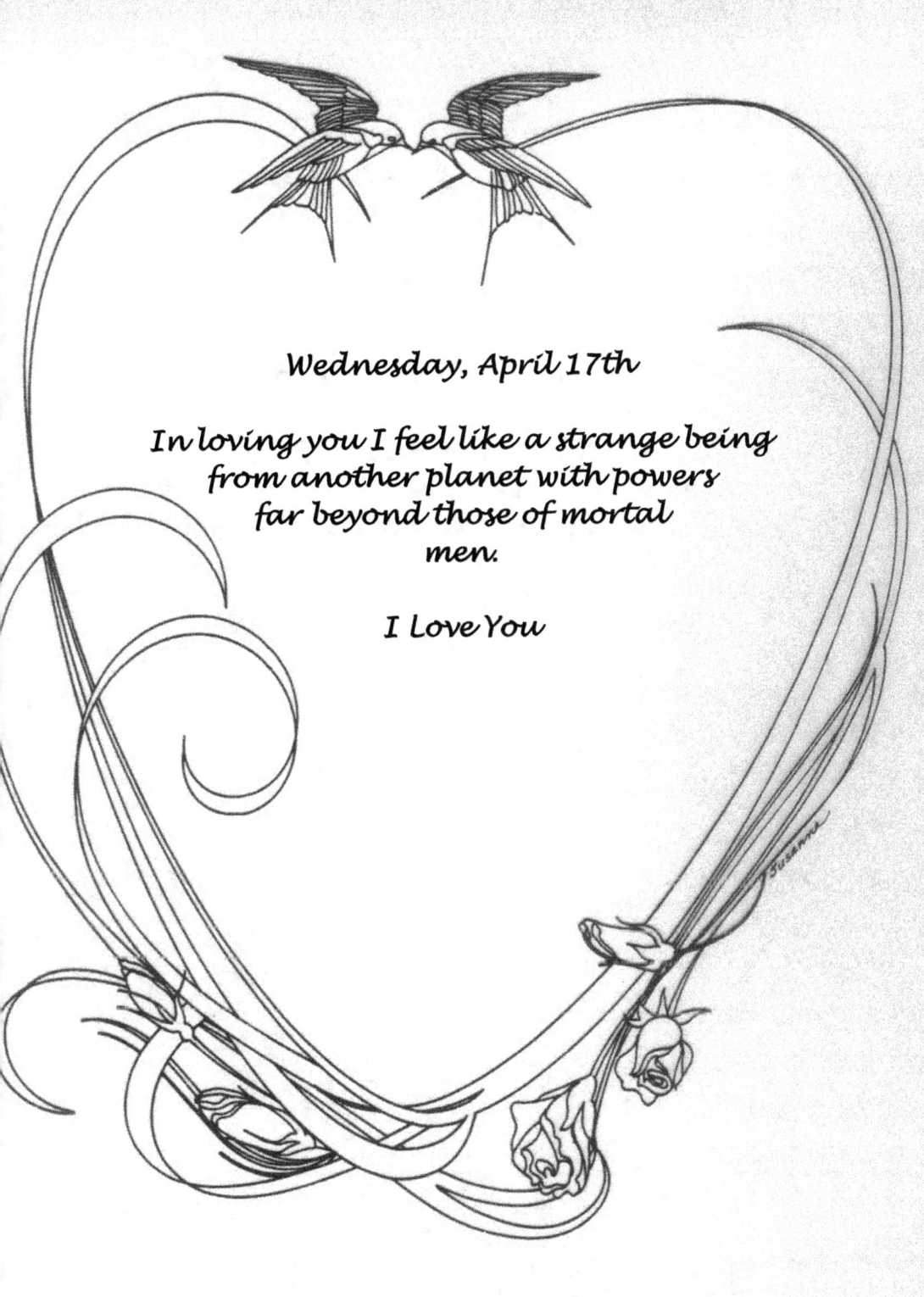

Wednesday, April 17th

In loving you I feel like a strange being
from another planet with powers
far beyond those of mortal
men.

I Love You

Thursday, April 18th

You are the personification of Absolute Love. Your very presence on Planet Earth is evidence of the Divinity in us all.

I Love You

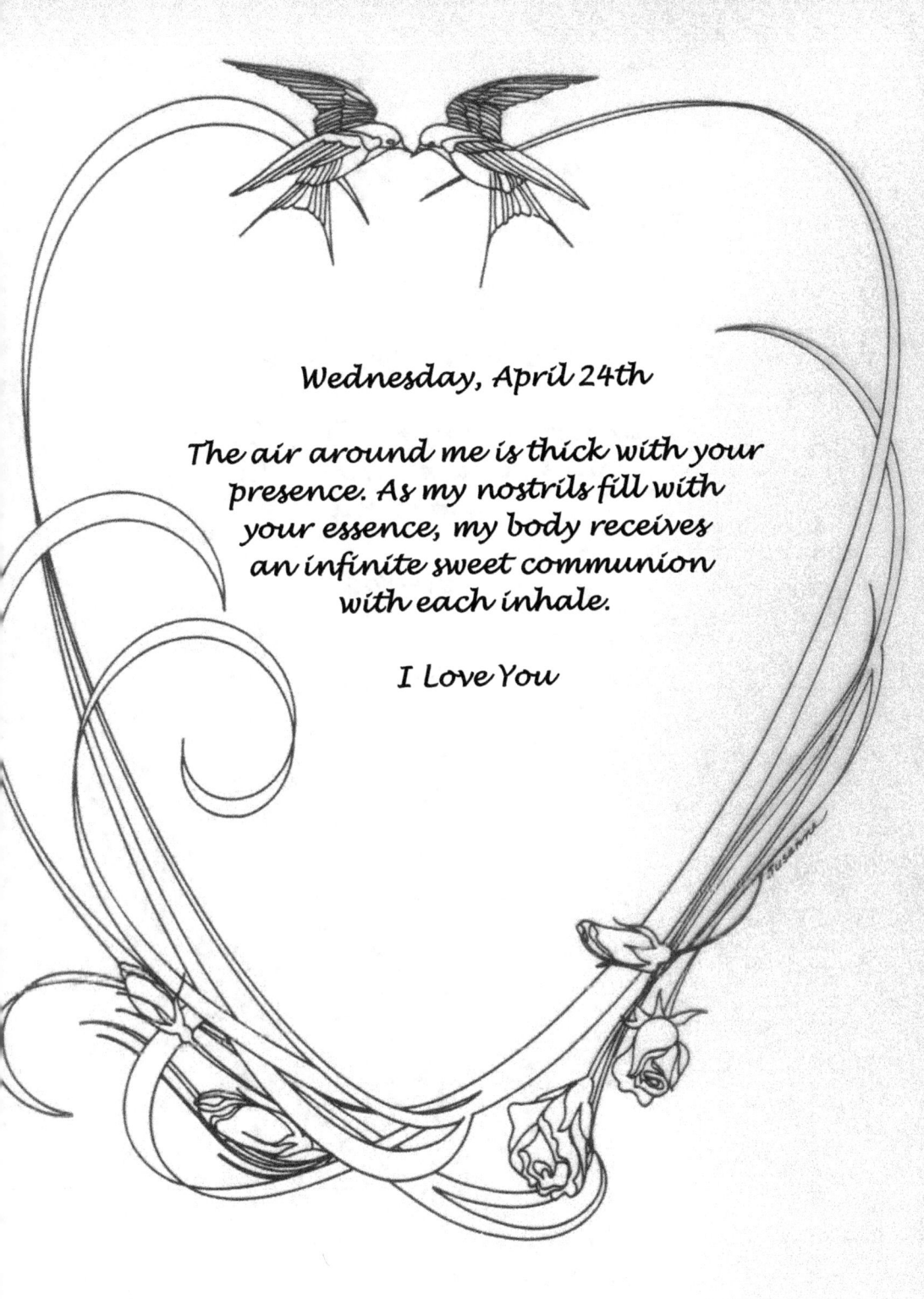

Wednesday, April 24th

The air around me is thick with your
presence. As my nostrils fill with
your essence, my body receives
an infinite sweet communion
with each inhale.

I Love You

Monday, April 29th

I am forever in your debt, for you
have saved me from a life
without you.

I Love You

Thursday, May 2nd

God so loved the world that he gave
me *You.* What a guy!

I Love You

Monday, May 6th

If there were no God, I would not only nominate you, I would be your campaign manager.

I Love You

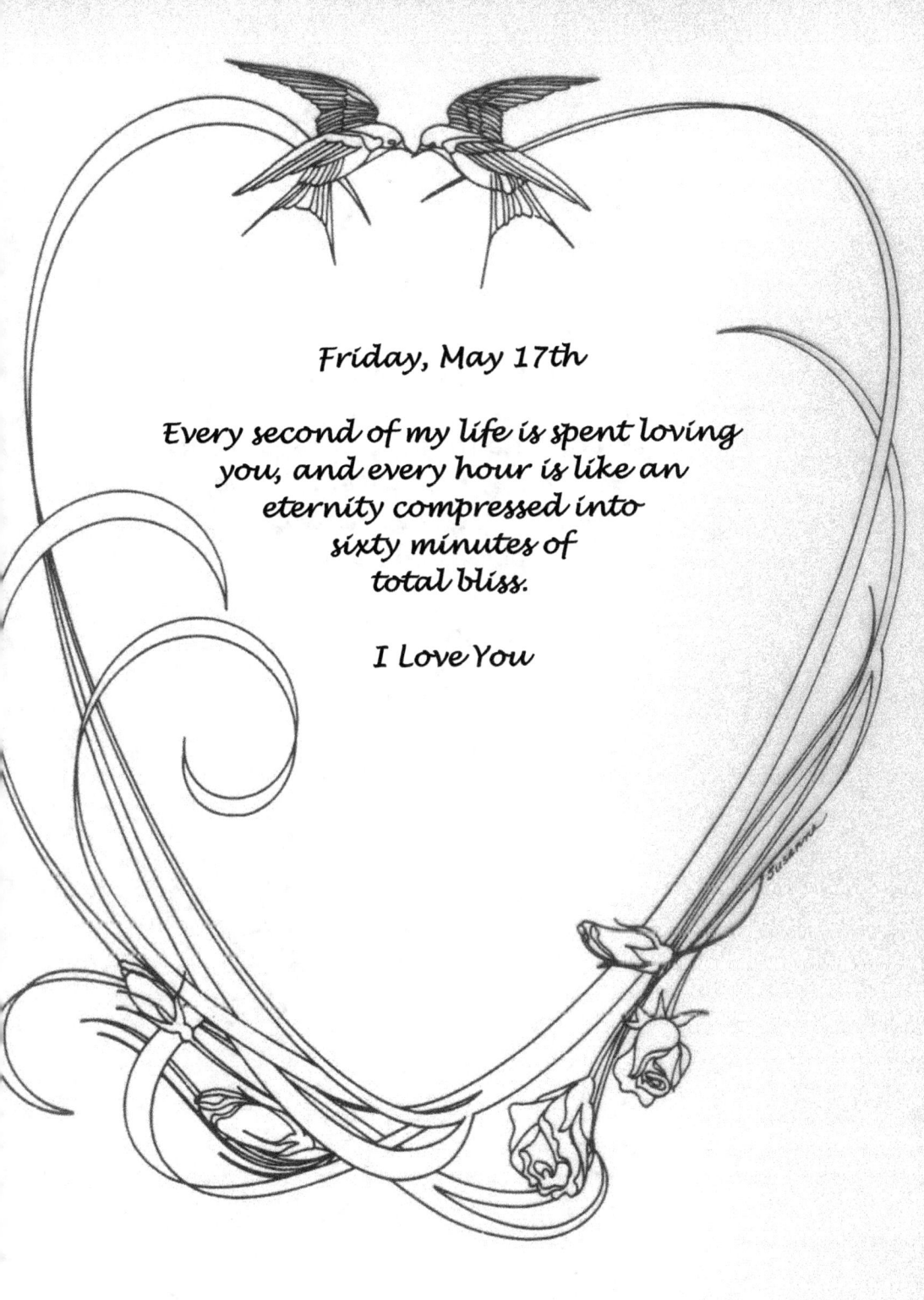

Friday, May 17th

Every second of my life is spent loving
you, and every hour is like an
eternity compressed into
sixty minutes of
total bliss.

I Love You

Tuesday, May 21st

It is impossible to deny the existence
of Goodness, Beauty and Love,
as you are these things
personified.

I Love You

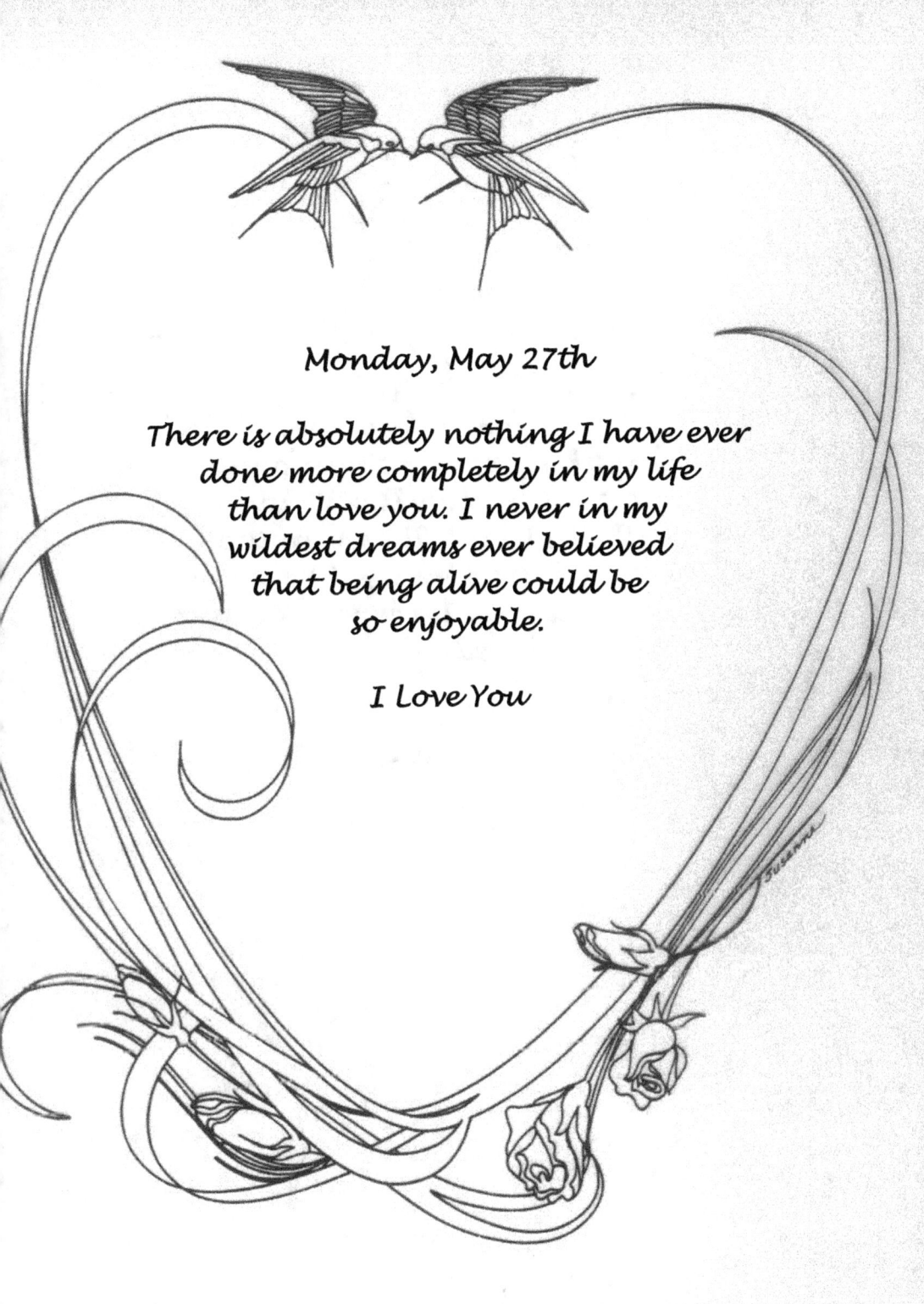

Monday, May 27th

There is absolutely nothing I have ever
done more completely in my life
than love you. I never in my
wildest dreams ever believed
that being alive could be
so enjoyable.

I Love You

Thursday, May 30th

When I was growing up, I wondered
what kind of woman I would
attract into my life. Would
she be beautiful, charming,
sensitive and sexy? You have
exceeded my expectations by
light years!

I Love You

Thursday, June 6th

In loving you I am experiencing such
a Oneness that I am beginning to
feel like a spiritual
hermaphrodite.

I Love You

Tuesday, June 11th

Universal Intelligence has a smile
stretching across the expanse of
its domain. It is watching you
in all your splendor, and it
is filled with delight.

I Love You

Friday, June 21st

Many, many, years ago in the land
of the timeless void, lived Queen Zona.
She ruled over everything that was,
is and will be. She was wise and
compassionate. All her subjects
loved her dearly. On April 13,
1946, Queen Zona entered the
land of time and space. Your
Grace, you are still wise
and compassionate.

I Love You

Tuesday, June 25th

Every molecule in my body loves every molecule in your body. This affliction is known as "Molecular Bliss." There is no cure, and as far as I know we are the only two people on Planet Earth who enjoy this condition.

I Love You

Wednesday, July 3rd

Eons ago in a galaxy far away, lived a
young Prince. One day his Princess
became lost in the land of time and
space. He was very saddened and
went to his father the King of the
Universe and asked for and was
granted permission to search
the land of time and space for
his princess. On 2-13-48 the
Prince assumed physical
form. 37 years later he found his
Princess. Now they are happy &
will one day return home.

I Love You Princess

Monday, July 8th

The most incomprehensible aspect of our human existence is love. It is the most widely talked about and least understood emotion we possess. Notwithstanding, I must confess that I have never enjoyed doing something I didn't understand as much as I have enjoyed doing it with you.

I Love You

Friday, July 12th

During a galactic phone call with the Unseen One last night, he told me who you really were. He said that you are the grandchild of Universal Mind; the daughter of Infinite Intelligence; and that God was your first cousin. Have I got some impressive in-laws or what?

I Love You

Friday, July 19th

I just wanted to take this opportunity to
thank you for creating such an
intelligent, gorgeous and
wonderful human being
and sharing her with
me.

I Love You

Tuesday, July 23rd

My love, if time were to stop this very instant, I would love you till the end of something else.

I Love You

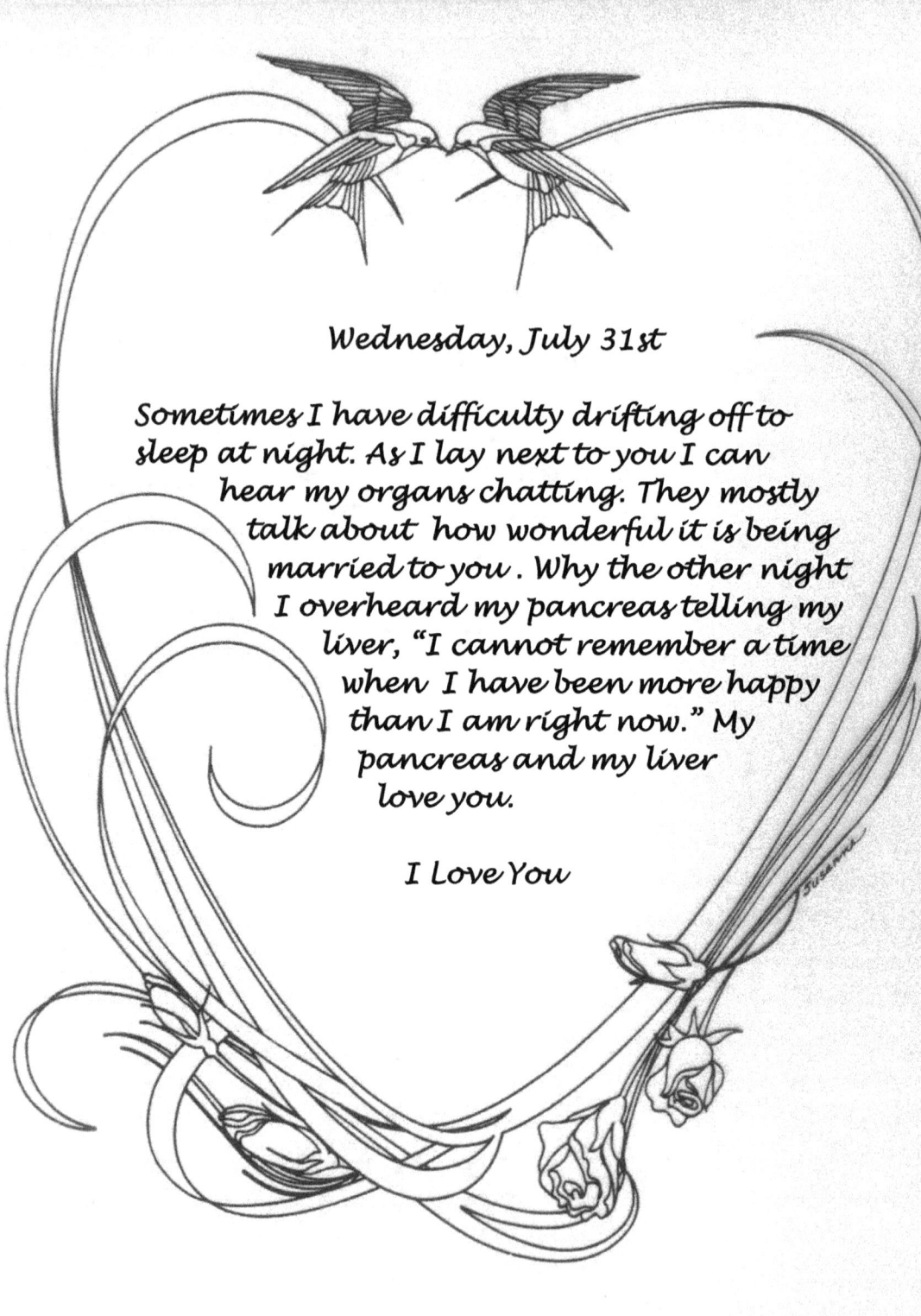

Wednesday, July 31st

Sometimes I have difficulty drifting off to sleep at night. As I lay next to you I can hear my organs chatting. They mostly talk about how wonderful it is being married to you. Why the other night I overheard my pancreas telling my liver, "I cannot remember a time when I have been more happy than I am right now." My pancreas and my liver love you.

I Love You

Thursday, August 1st

As I am writing this morning, I can hear
you in the other room doing your morn-
ing stuff. It dawns on me that you are
less than twenty feet from me, and I
can go to you right now, if I
choose, and hold you in my arms,
kiss you and tell you how very
much I love you. Life is good!

I Love You

Tuesday August 6th

As the Gods look approvingly down upon us, they see the perfect manifestation of Universal Intelligence. Next month you and I will be inducted into the Cosmic Human Being Hall Of Fame. Only humans who have experienced total and absolute bliss are nominated. Wear something nice.

I Love You

Friday, August 9th

You are the Rolls Royce of Human Beings. Hand made by Universal Intelligence.

I Love You

Monday, August 19th

I revel in every nanosecond I spend within
your Morphogenetic Energy Field. You
are the result of Divine Formative
Causation whose total embodi-
ment I have the ultimate
honor of experiencing
everyday for the rest
of Eternity.

I Love You

Thursday, August 29th

There was a time when the Universe had no
physical form. There was no Milky Way,
and God was just learning fractions.
At this point in time I had already
loved you 1,000,000,000,000 years.
Our love has clearly withstood
the test of time.

I Love You

Friday, August 30th

You are the essence of Universal Matter. All neutrons, protons and electrons await your beck and call. You created the Universe on a Monday morning with a snap of your finger. You created the Milky Way in a dream while taking a nap. However, the creation that dwarfs all others by comparison is <u>You</u>! Thanks for doing such a magnificent job.

I Love You

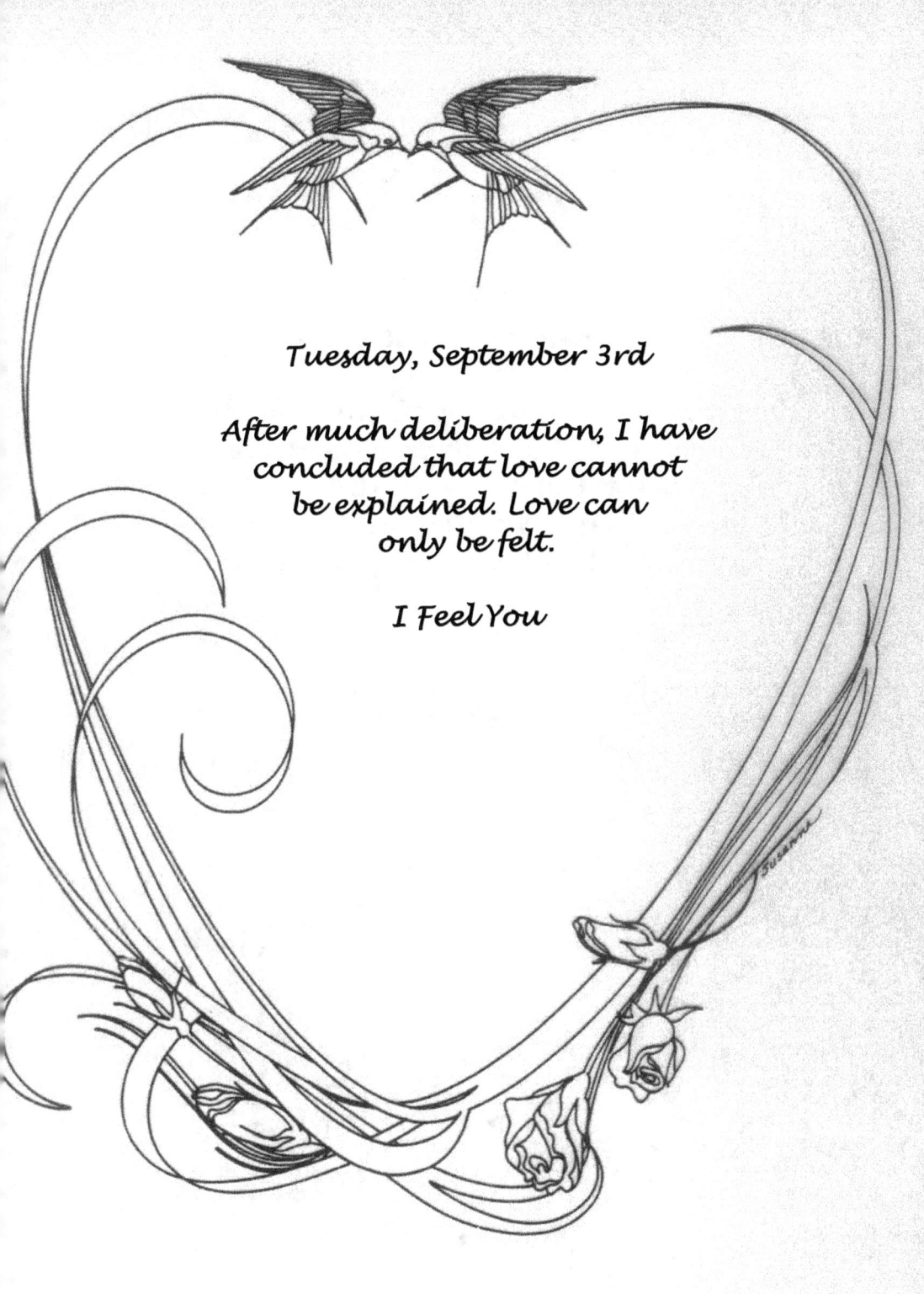

Tuesday, September 3rd

After much deliberation, I have
concluded that love cannot
be explained. Love can
only be felt.

I Feel You

Wednesday, September 11th

I am so in love with you! There I go
being happier than I was yesterday.
And, tomorrow I will be happier
than I was today. You know,
I think I am beginning to
understand infinity.

I Love You

Friday, September 20th

I love you so much that not only is
there not enough words to describe
this love, but not enough paper
in the Universe to write it on.
The one thing there is
enough of is You!

I Love You

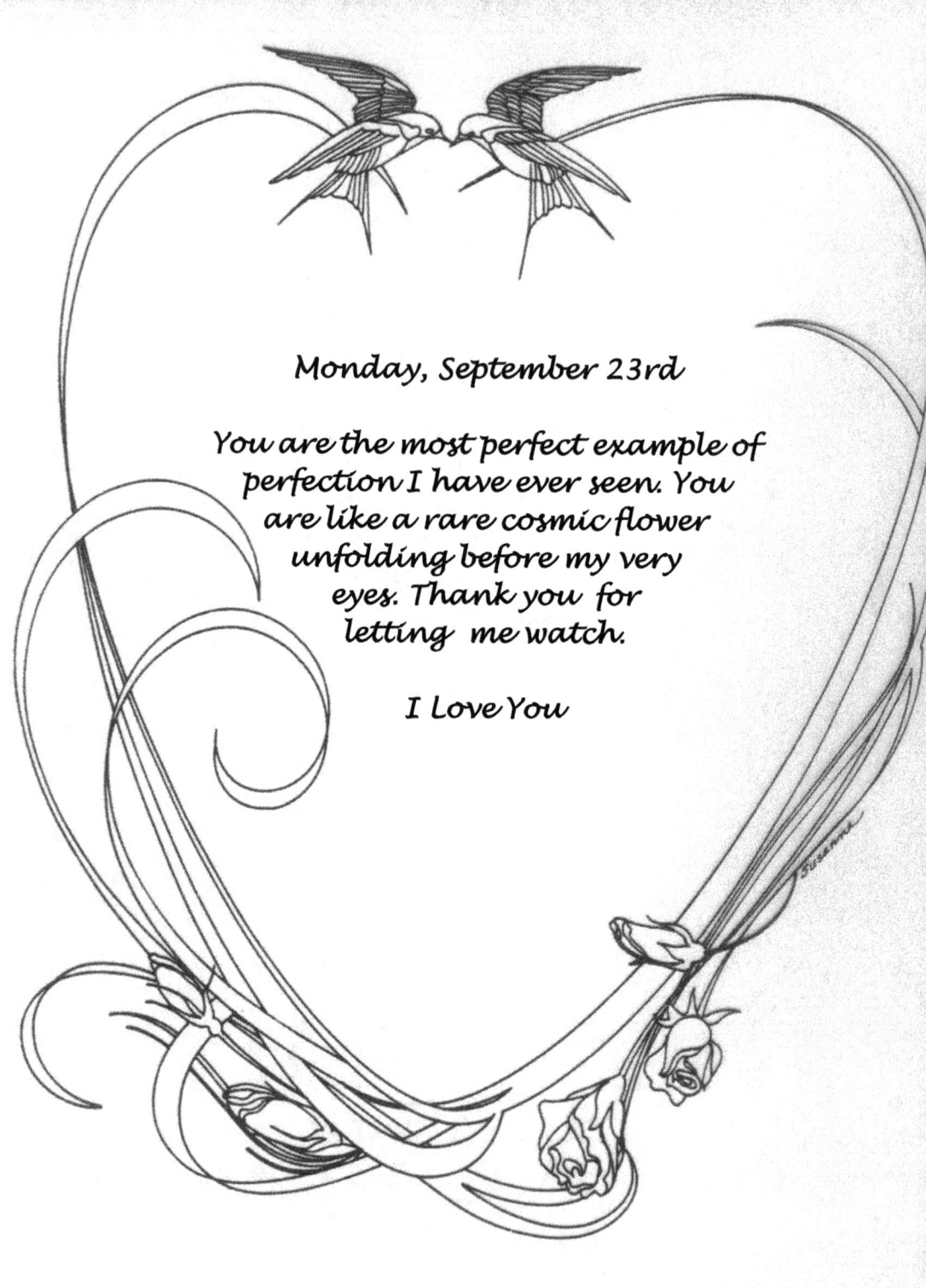

Monday, September 23rd

You are the most perfect example of perfection I have ever seen. You are like a rare cosmic flower unfolding before my very eyes. Thank you for letting me watch.

I Love You

Thursday, September 26th

The Universal Force that created you,
is the same Force that created
beautiful sunsets, the Mona
Lisa and NY cheesecake.

I Love You

Monday, September 30th

During my conversation with the Unseen
One last night, I told him all about you.
I told him you are gorgeous, intell-
igent, charming, loving, caring,
sweet, adorable, lovely, an excellent
cook, and a magnificent lover. He
responded, "That's funny, my
wife is exactly like that too."

I Love You

Wednesday, October 2nd

I am happy that you are feeling better to-
day. I sometimes feel like the curator
of the most valuable work of art
ever created, and whenever you
are experiencing disharmony
our Universe is affected accord-
ingly. I can now rest assured
that peace and harmony are
once again restored to our
Universe.

I Love You

Tuesday, October 8th

From a mire of apathy and emptiness arose a Consciousness that had lain dormant since the beginning of Creation. That Consciousness is now in our possession, and its influence will change the course of human destiny. Do you think my Ego needs a reality check?

I Love You

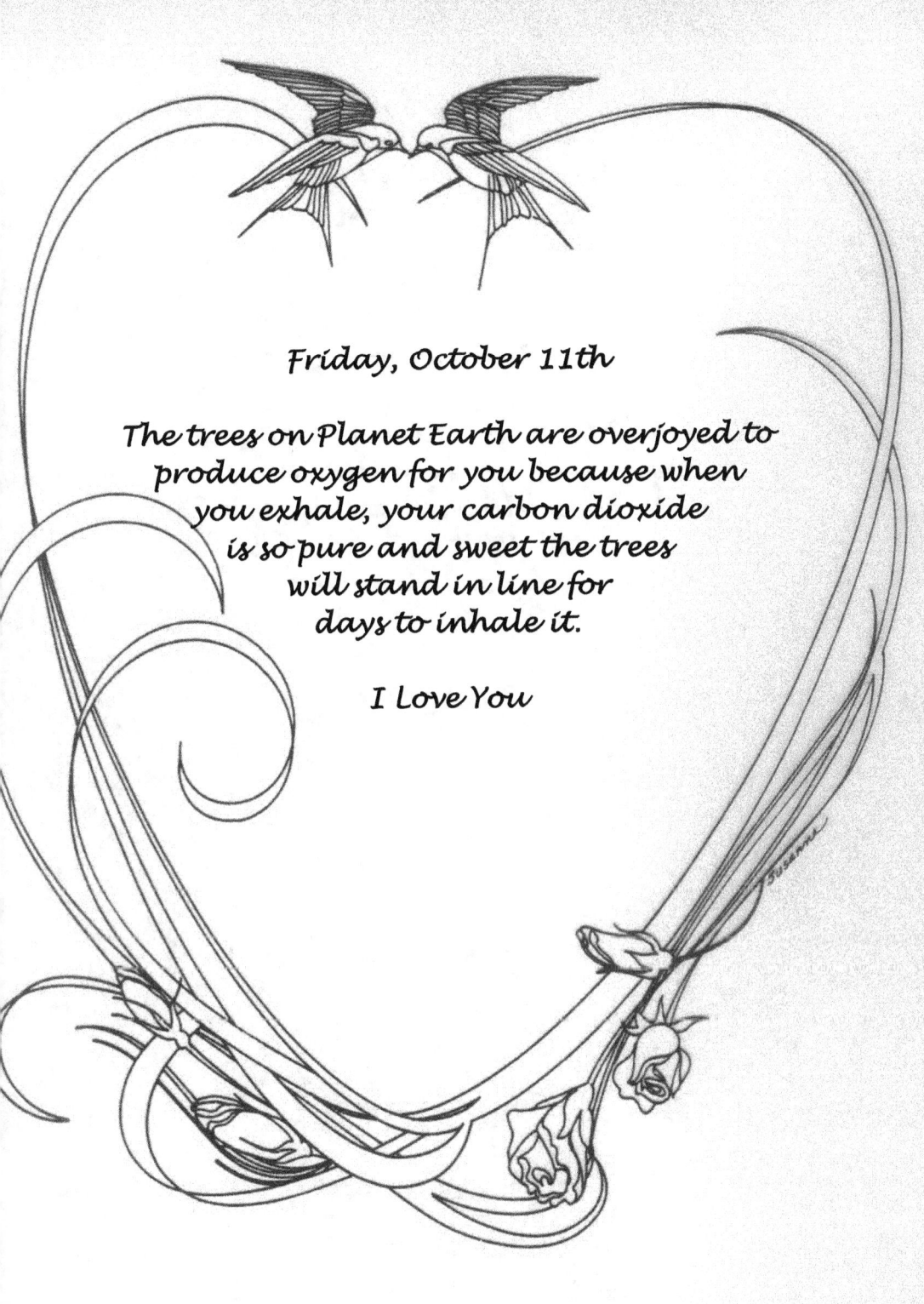

Friday, October 11th

The trees on Planet Earth are overjoyed to
produce oxygen for you because when
you exhale, your carbon dioxide
is so pure and sweet the trees
will stand in line for
days to inhale it.

I Love You

Monday, October 14th

Last night I had a dream that you and I were very much in love and that we were living happily ever after. Isn't it wonderful living a dream come true?

I Love You

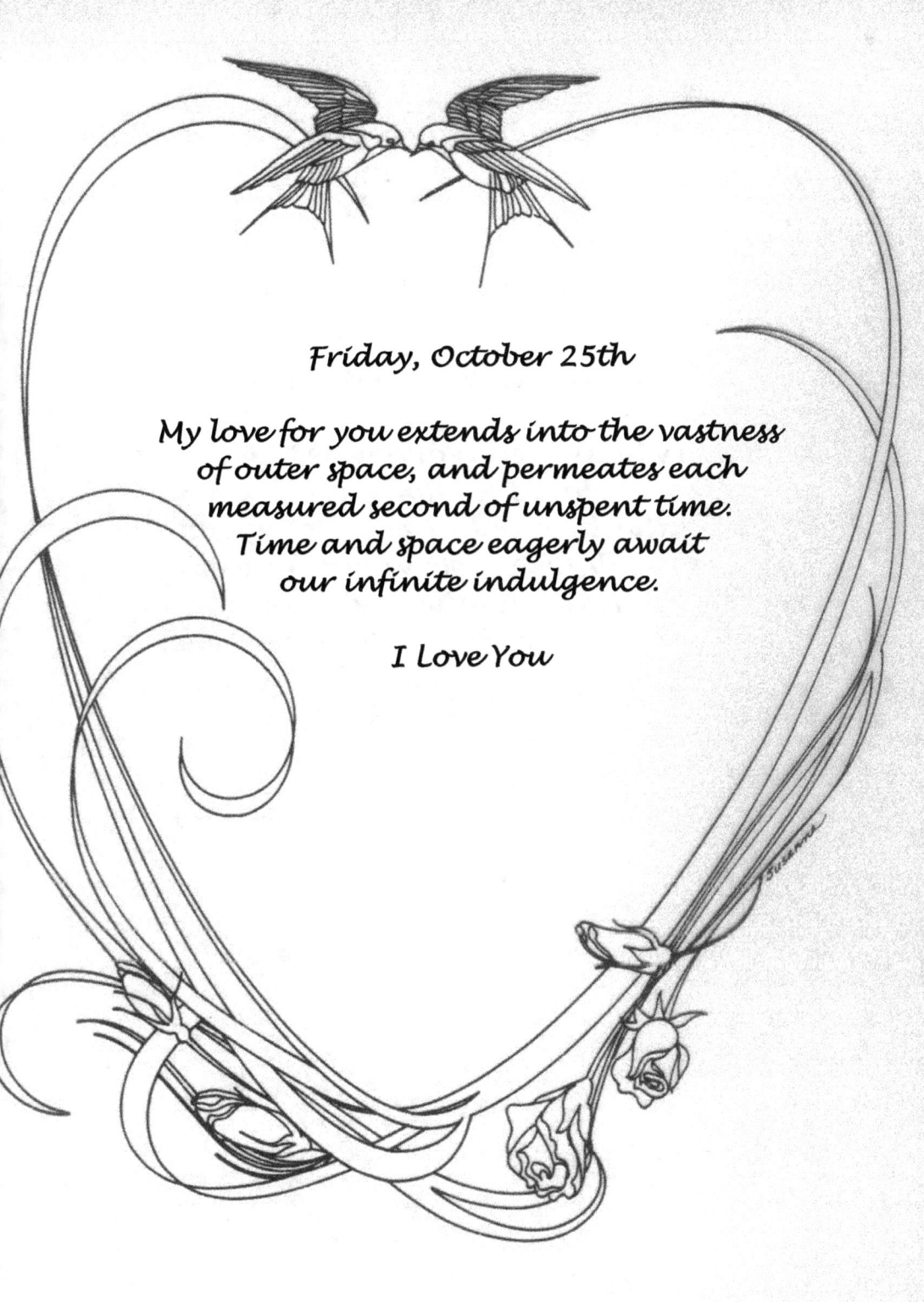

Friday, October 25th

My love for you extends into the vastness
of outer space, and permeates each
measured second of unspent time.
Time and space eagerly await
our infinite indulgence.

I Love You

Thursday, October 31st

If every living being on Planet Earth could
feel the love I feel for you right now,
all wars would immediately stop,
all sick people would instantly
heal and the world's population
would double in nine months.

I Love You

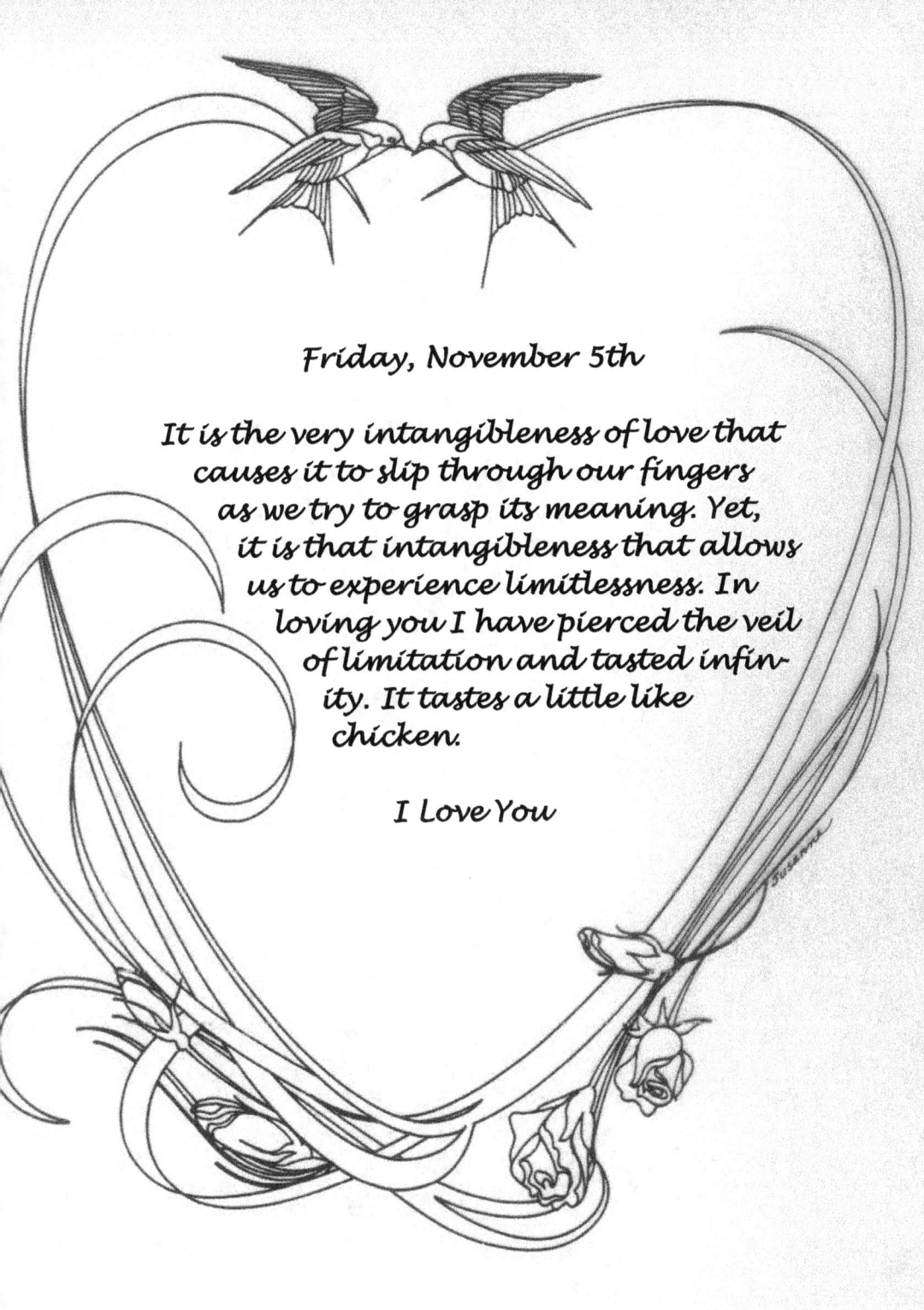

Friday, November 5th

It is the very intangibleness of love that
causes it to slip through our fingers
as we try to grasp its meaning. Yet,
it is that intangibleness that allows
us to experience limitlessness. In
loving you I have pierced the veil
of limitation and tasted infin-
ity. It tastes a little like
chicken.

I Love You

Friday, November 8th

After considerable thought, I have concluded that in loving you I am able to love myself, and that it is not adversity that introduces a man to himself, but love.

I Love You

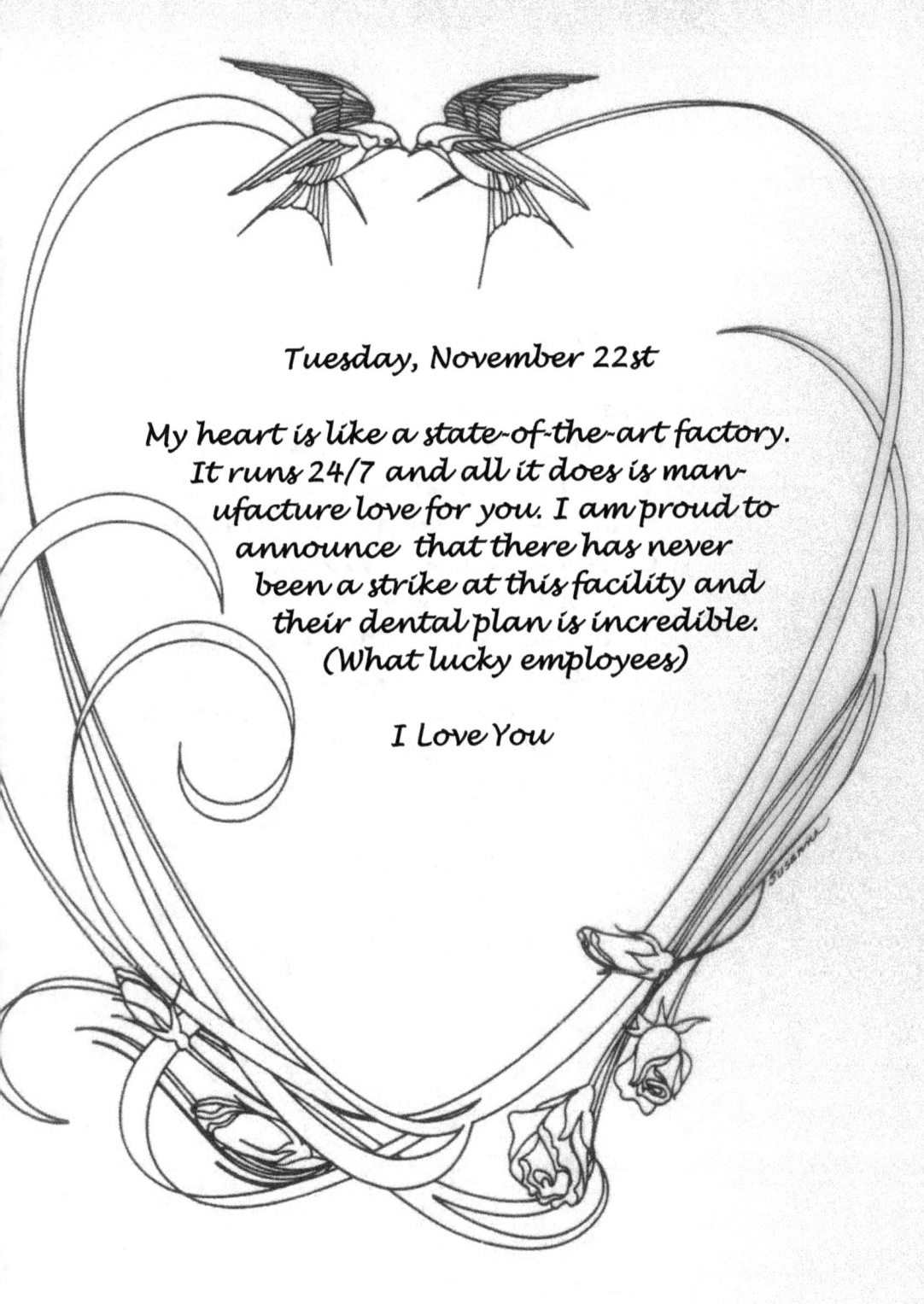

Tuesday, November 22st

My heart is like a state-of-the-art factory. It runs 24/7 and all it does is man- ufacture love for you. I am proud to announce that there has never been a strike at this facility and their dental plan is incredible. (What lucky employees)

I Love You

Thursday, November 21st

Last night I astral projected to the planet Zentron. Its inhabitants were in mourning, and had been since April 12, 1946. I reassured them that their Queen was alive and well. They all rejoiced at the news, and began a celebration that will end upon your arrival home. They asked if I would accompany you. I replied, "Absolutely." Your Majesty, our happiness will continue into infinity.

I Love You

Friday, November 29th

While in your embrace, I melt into a
peaceful Oneness where time and
space cease to exist. Your arms
are an infinite vacuum
where I find blissful
sanctuary.

I Love You

Wednesday, December 4th

Of all the treasures I have discovered through my journey on this plane, you are without a doubt the most precious. To equate your worth in dollars would take every printing press on Planet Earth running 24/7 for a trillion years to print up enough money to buy the toe nail on one of your little toes.

I Love You

Monday, December 9th

I truly envy my Subconscious Mind.
Because of you, it has recorded
and stored some of the most
wonderful experiences ever
experienced by a Conscious
Mind.

I Love You

Thursday, December 12th

Sometimes when I look at you I think
of a line from one my favorite
songs. "How I won you I
shall never never know."

I Love You

Friday, December 27th

As the Gods look down upon us, they
are very pleased at what they see.
They see Love, Compassion, Joy,
Health, Abundance, Peace, and
Harmony. As they leave, they are
patting themselves on the back.

I Love You

Tuesday, December 31st

The echoes of our embrace reverberates
through my entire Being until every
molecule is engulfed with your infi-
nite essence. My molecules cannot
wait to come home from the office
everyday so the process can
start anew.

I Love You

Thursday, January 2nd

I wonder if you have any idea how much
I love you? I'll let you know when I
have finished counting. So far, I
have counted all the stars in the
Heavens, and am now counting
all the atoms in the Universe.
I may be late for dinner.

I Love You

Wednesday, January 8th

Sometimes I feel like the winner of the
Universe's Grand Opening contest
several billion years ago, and
that you are the last installment
of the prize I won.

I Love You

Friday, January 24th

Upon returning from my astral journey
early this morning, all my suspicions
about you were confirmed. I was
informed by the Supreme Source
that you are indeed the perfect
manifestation of Universal
Intelligence.

I Love You

Tuesday, January 28th

My love for you is so enormous,
I haven't finished visualizing
it yet.

I Love You

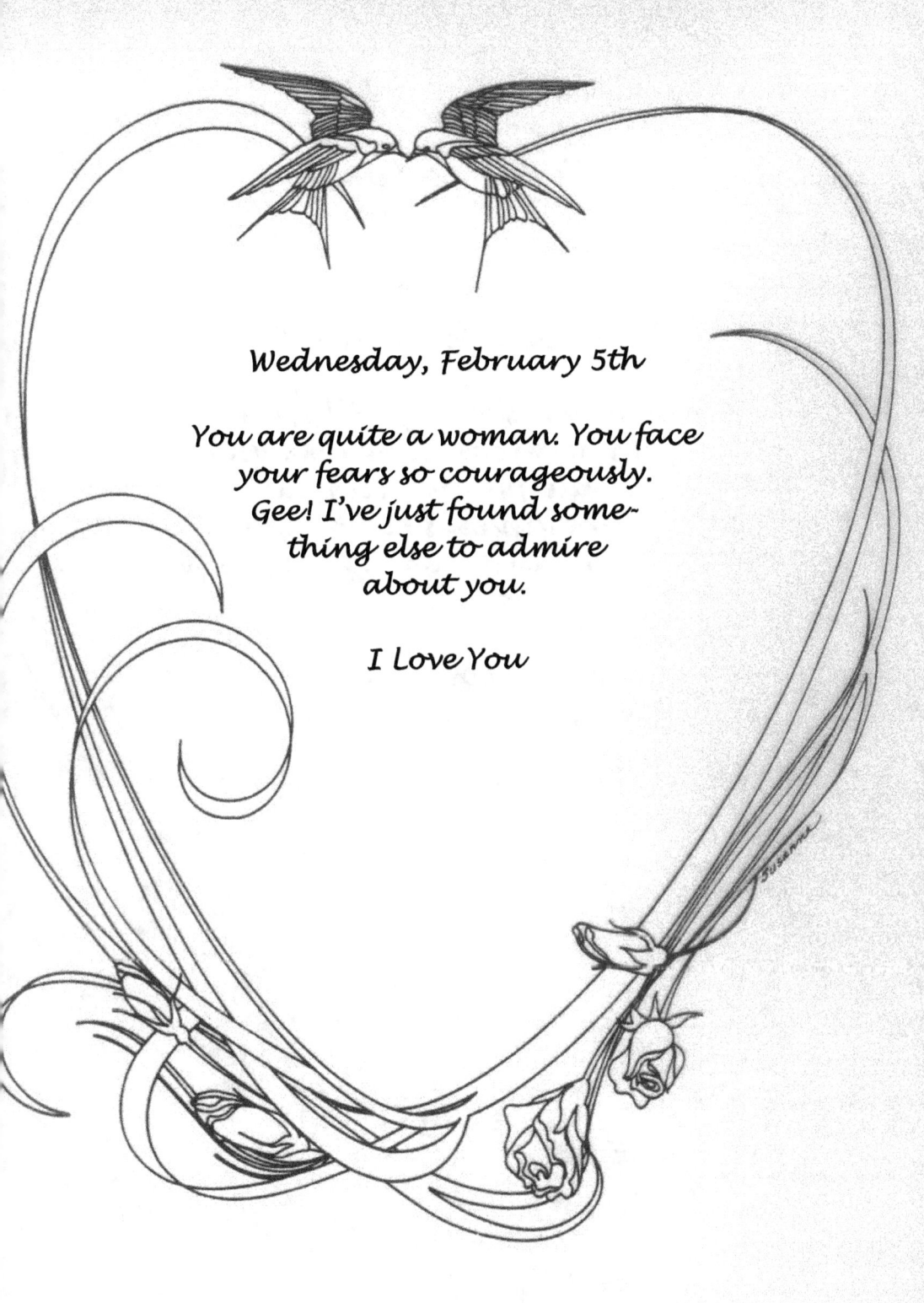

Wednesday, February 5th

*You are quite a woman. You face
your fears so courageously.
Gee! I've just found some-
thing else to admire
about you.*

I Love You

Monday, February 10th

Loving you is such a joyful experience that whenever I think about how wonderful you are, I must contain my smile because there isn't enough room on my face.

I Love You

Thursday, February 13th

I've just taken all of my vitamins and the
biggest and most important vitamin
I take everyday is <u>You</u>. The dose is
administered through the eyes. So,
the next time you catch me staring
into your gorgeous eyes, know that
my molecules are rejoicing as
they receive an Infinite
Communion of the purest
love in our Universe.

I Love You

Monday, March 3rd

What a treasure you are. A treasure
that was hidden in my future. If
I had known about you I could
have started being the happiest
man in the Universe a long time
ago.

I Love You

Thursday, March 6th

There is a solar system far away where perfection is taken for granted. The people live in peace, harmony and love. There are no wars or politicians. There is no sugar, salt or meat on this planet, only fruits, vegetables and garlic. Echoes from time and space beckon us to return home. Will you leave with me tonight?

I Love You

Tuesday, March 11th

Since man first learned to write, there has never been documentation recorded anywhere of any human being that was as happy as I am with you. These written words are the first ever of anyone achieving total happiness.

I Love You

Monday, March 17th

I have a perpetual smile on my face, even when I am not physically smiling. It can only be seen when you look into my eyes. There, you can see my Soul, and it is gig-gling like a 5 year old.

I Love You

Wednesday, March 19th

At Her last press conference, God was questioned about us. She just smiled because She knew.

I Love You

Tuesday, March 25th

Has there ever been a time when
I did not love you?

Yes _____   No ___X___

I Love You

Tuesday, April 8th

You are, without a doubt, the loveliest woman ever created. In fact, they didn't break the mold when they made you, they saved it and stored it in a cosmic vault somewhere in the Milky Way. Its location is still a secret to this day.

I Love You

Friday, April 11th

I just marvel at my capacity to love you.
I have gotten so good at loving you
that if there was an Olympic event
called "Loving Susan Solivan", I
would win the gold metal every
four years for the rest of eternity.

I Love You

Thursday, April 25th

On a scale from 1 to 10, I would say
you are a 1,000,000,000,000.

I Love You

Tuesday, April 29th

When you and I leave this plane of
existence we will travel the
Universe, Galaxy by Galaxy. I
will take you to the God of your
understanding. He will be
delighted to see His most
favorite creation once
again. <u>You</u>!

I Love You

Tuesday, May 6th

Before you were created, there were no stars. Your creation lit up the Heavens as if a giant light switch had been turned on. If it weren't for you lovers would have no-where to go to make out.

I Love You

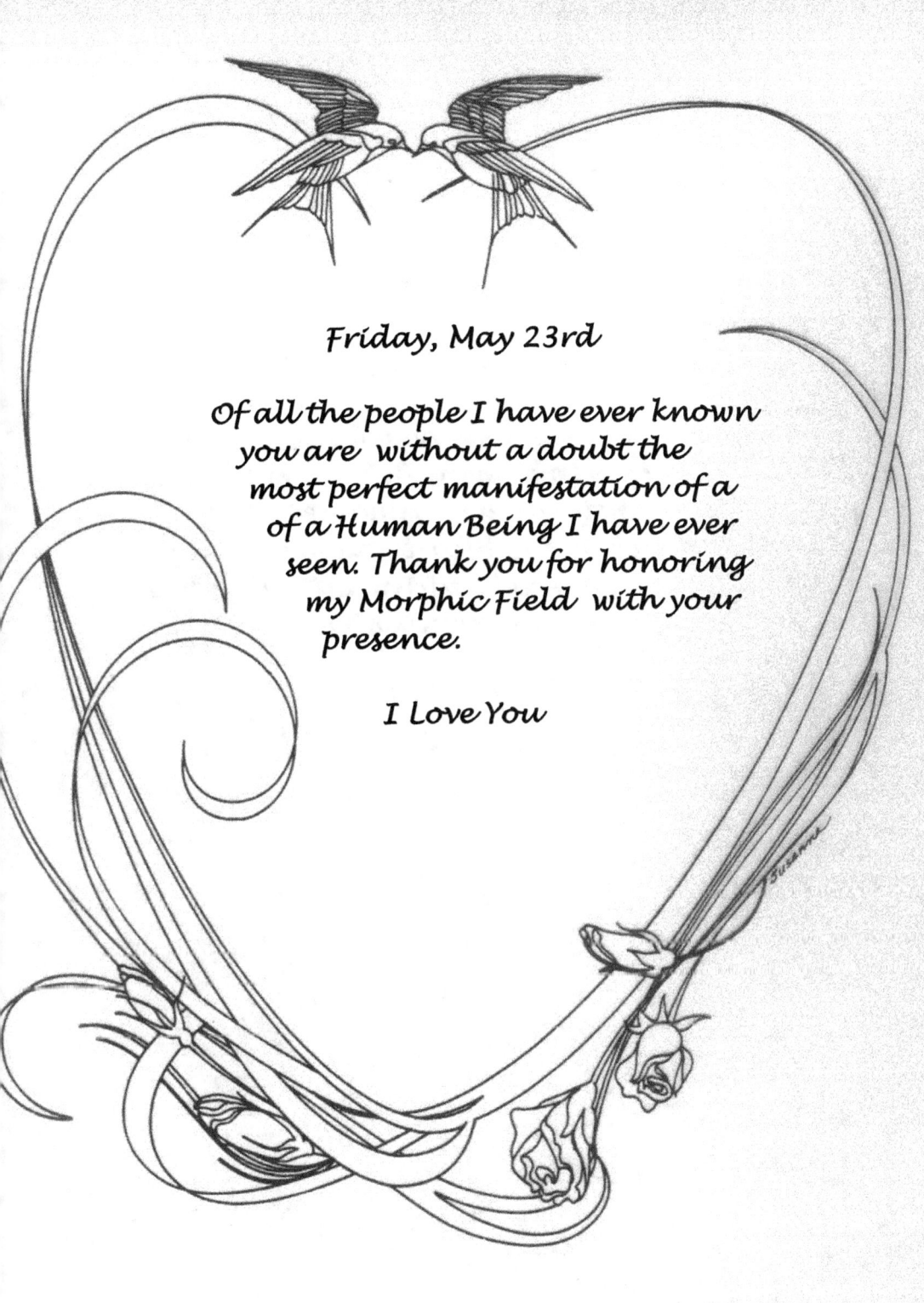

Friday, May 23rd

Of all the people I have ever known
you are without a doubt the
most perfect manifestation of a
of a Human Being I have ever
seen. Thank you for honoring
my Morphic Field with your
presence.

I Love You

Monday, May 26th

You have taken my heart on a delightful journey to dimensions reserved only for the Gods. I am one of the privileged few to have actually experienced Infinity. What do you do for an encore?

I Love You

Friday, May 30th

To have found you among 4 billion people
is the greatest fortune to have befallen
any living creature since dark found
light. Every breath I take is a
reminder that I will live another
few seconds to experience _You_.

I Love You

Thursday, June 19th

Every morning as I awaken, I look over and see you lying next to me. It gives me such profound joy because at that moment I realize that the day before was not a dream. Whatever you do today, please don't pinch me.

I Love You

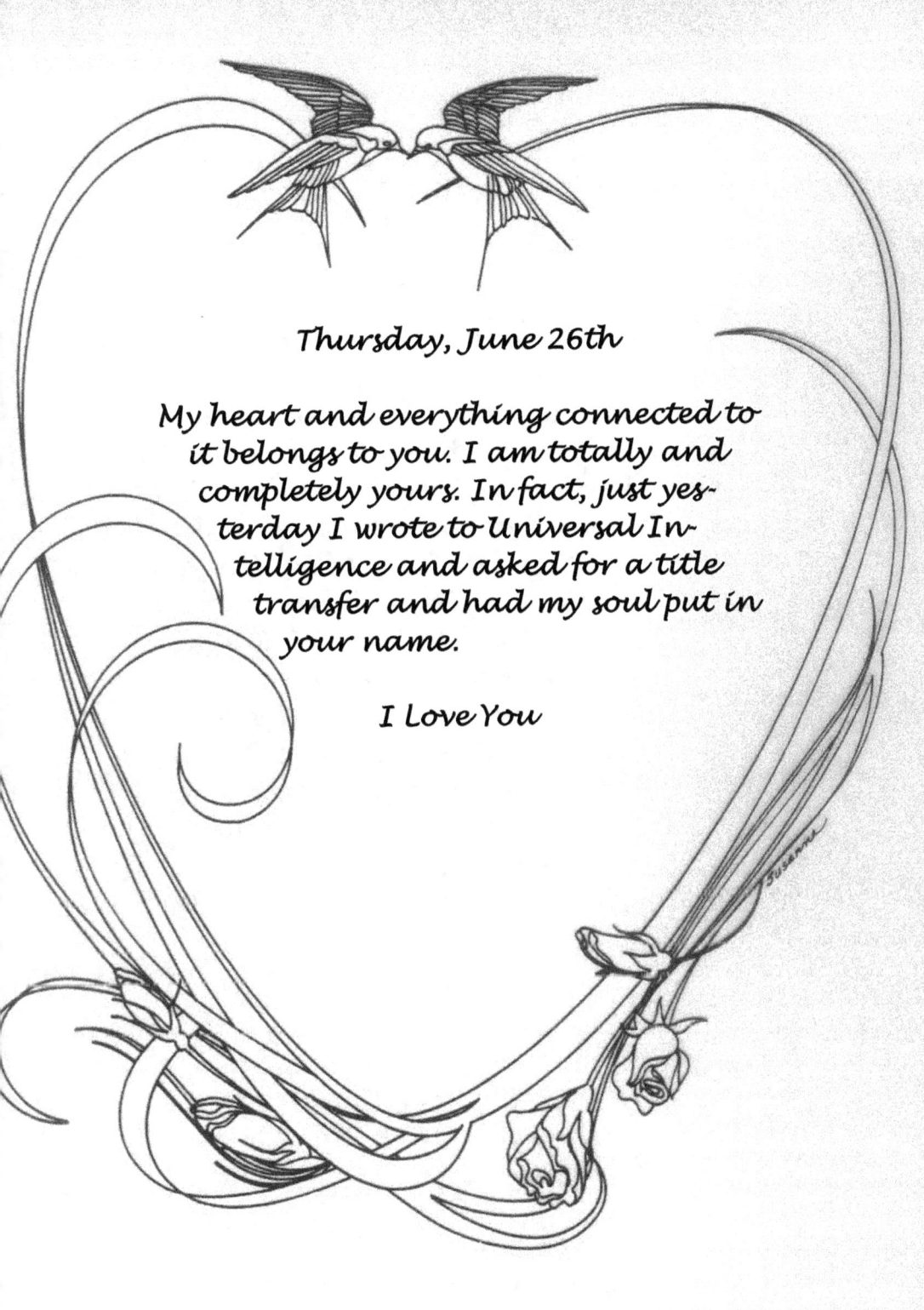

Thursday, June 26th

My heart and everything connected to it belongs to you. I am totally and completely yours. In fact, just yesterday I wrote to Universal Intelligence and asked for a title transfer and had my soul put in your name.

I Love You

Monday, June 30th

There once lived a King name Zoltar. He was the ruler of the Universe in the 4th Quadrant. His queen's name was Zeta. She was the most beautiful God Being ever to create herself. In the year of Existential Denial they were separated. On 4-13-46 Zoltar heard that his Queen had surfaced in the 7th Quadrant. On 2-13-48 Zoltar assumed physical form and was reunited with his Queen. Don't you just love happy endings?

I Love You

Monday, July 7th

I was speaking, at length, with Universal Mind last night. He asked me how everything was going, and I said great. He then told me that he would have gotten us together a lot sooner, but there were problems in the middle east, inflation, gas shortages, etc. The reason he was able to get us together now was because the 80's were pretty quiet.

I Love You

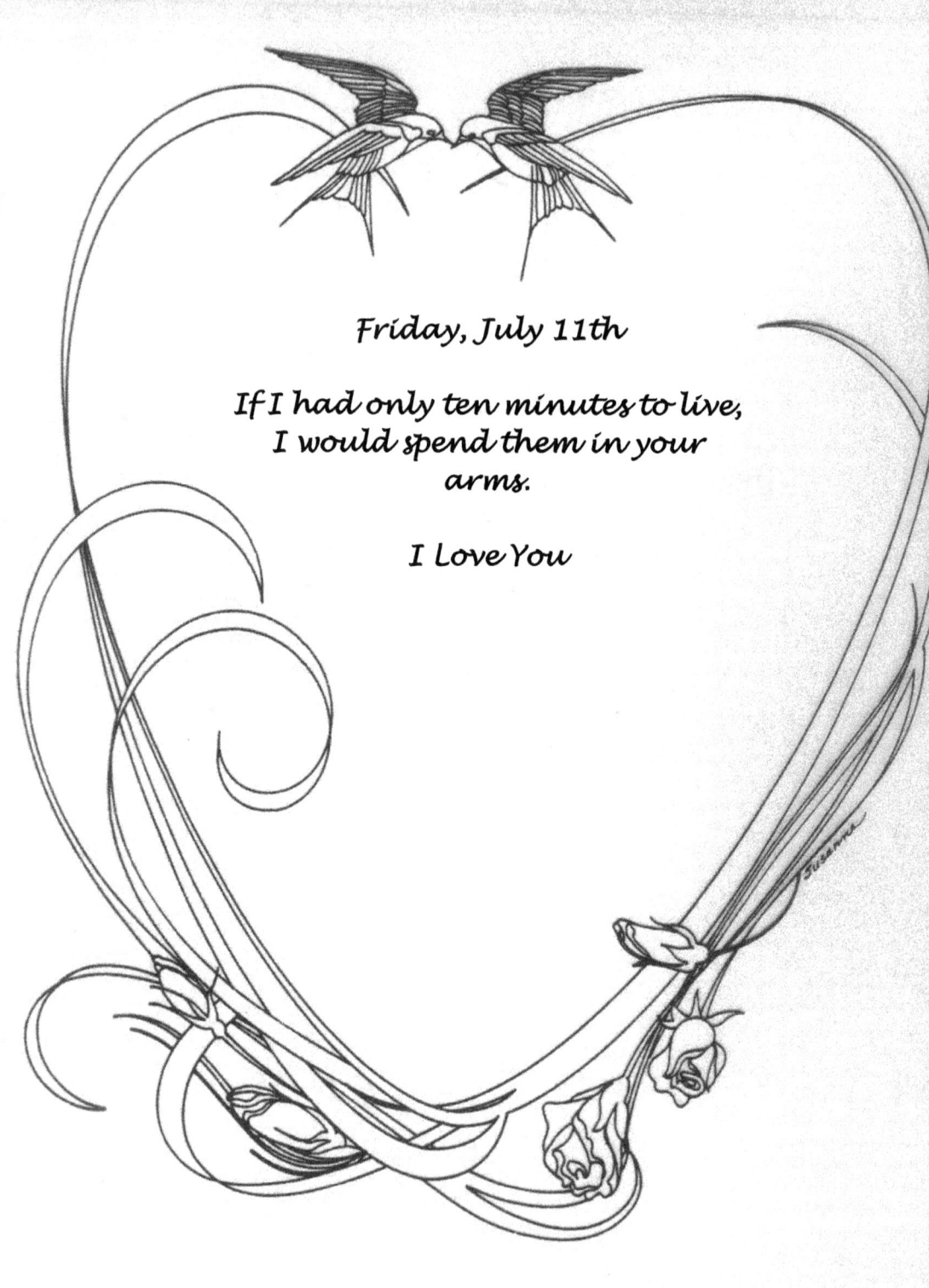

Friday, July 11th

If I had only ten minutes to live,
I would spend them in your
arms.

I Love You

Tuesday, July 15th

To know you and not love you
is abnormal.

I Love You

Monday, July 28th

To have been allowed to live and not
love you is something for which
I would have never forgiven
our creator.

I Love You

Tuesday, August 5th

When all else has turned to dust and blown away, our love will still be there. Our love is so unalterable that it will survive in a vacuum. At this very moment physicists around the world are scratching their heads trying to explain this phenomenon.

I Love You

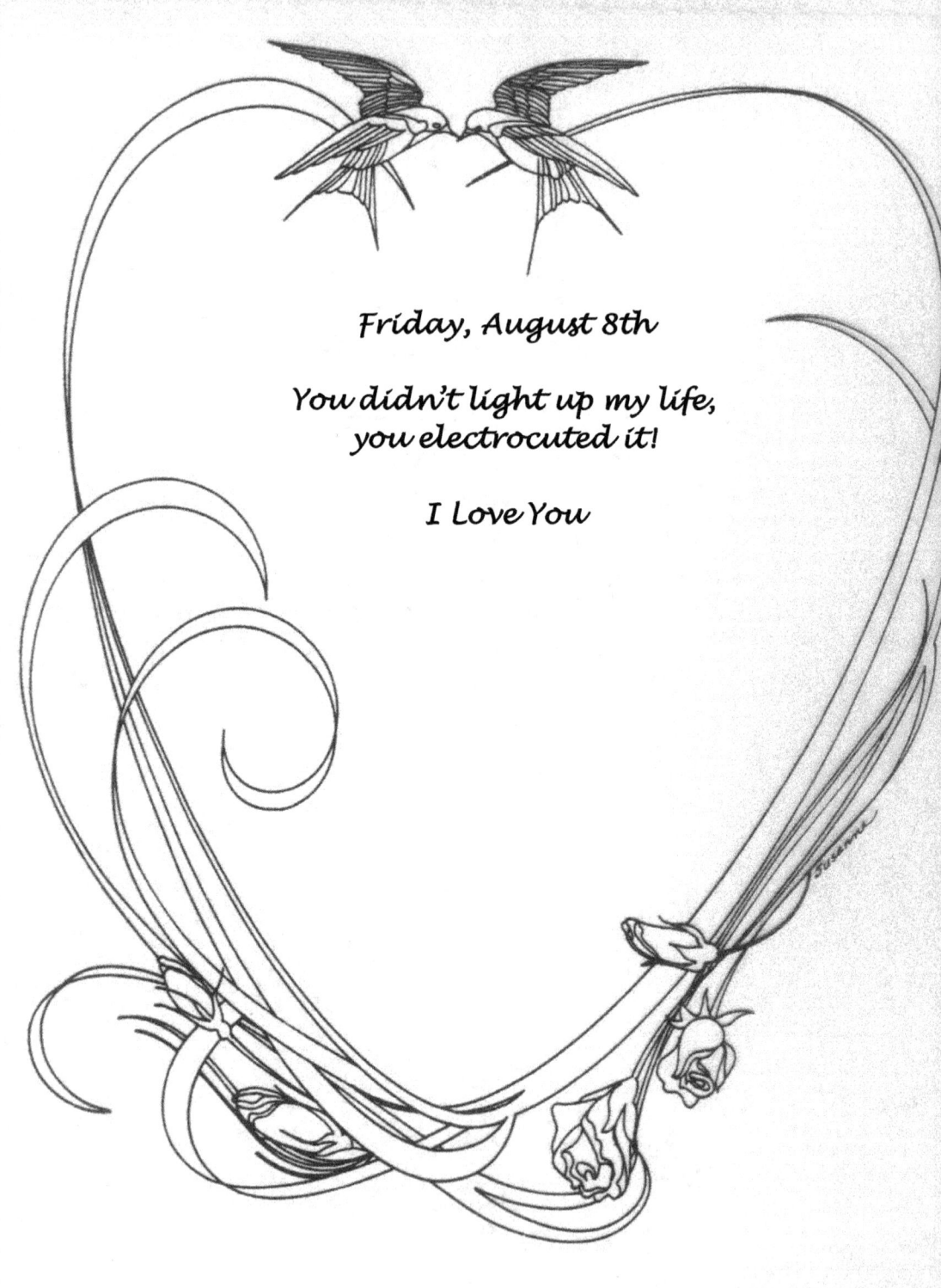

Friday, August 8th

You didn't light up my life,
you electrocuted it!

I Love You

Tuesday, August 12th

You are an angel sent to me from the
God of Happiness. Sometimes I think
that one day I may be looking
through your closet and find
a pair of wings.

I Love You

Thursday, August 14th

*In loving you, I am literally astounded
at my capacity to love and my
good fortune of having you
in my life. You have filled
my life with life.*

I Love You

Monday, August 25th

Your love has swallowed
me whole.

I Love You

Wednesday, September 24th

You are every beautiful experience
that has ever happened to me
rolled up into one lovely
and exquisite package.

I Love You

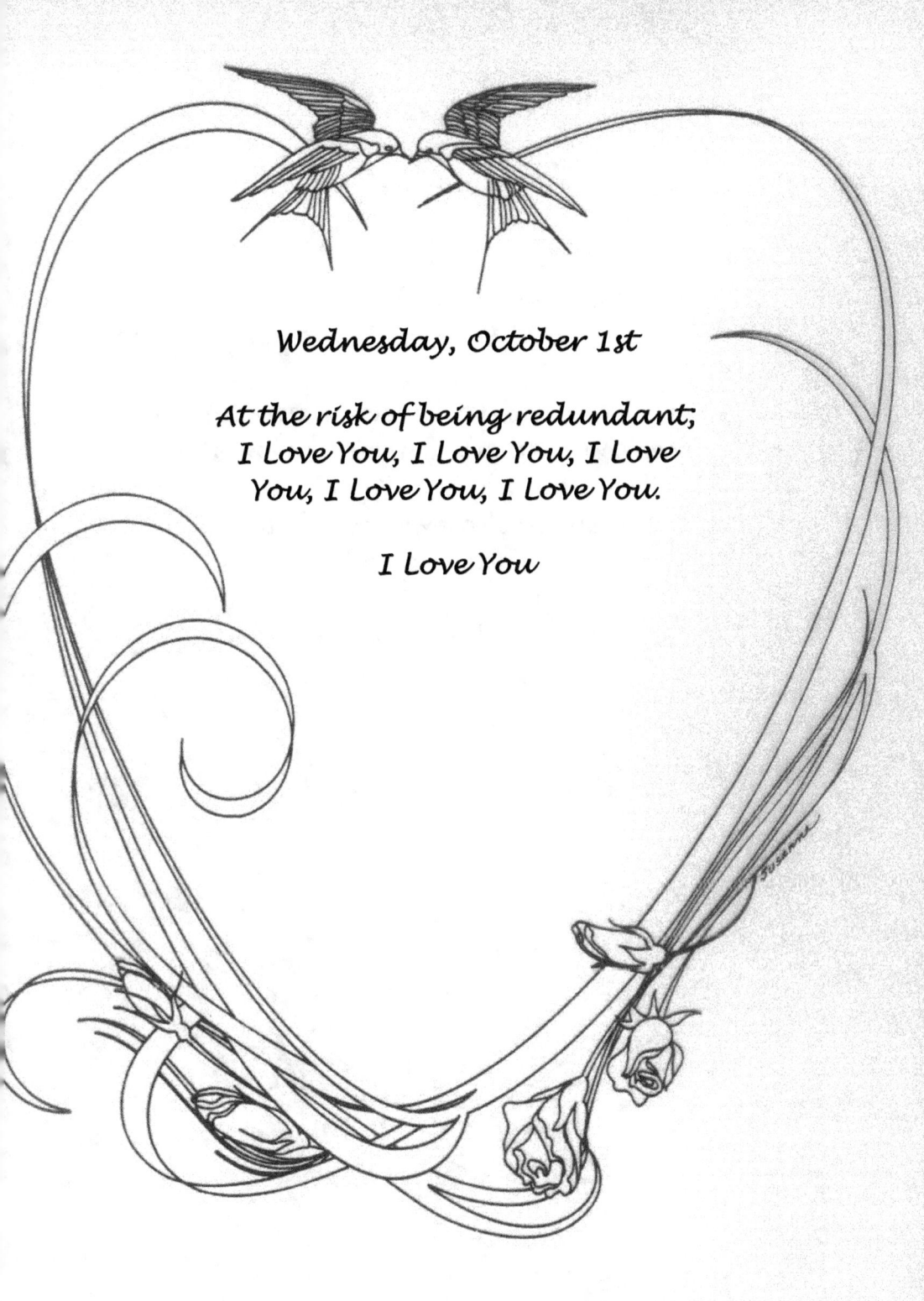

Wednesday, October 1st

At the risk of being redundant,
I Love You, I Love You, I Love
You, I Love You, I Love You.

I Love You

Tuesday, October 7th

Your love and its reverberations per-
meate my total consciousness with
a warmth and joy that is
surely the essence of all
that is good.

I Love You

Thursday, October 16th

I am so in love with you that when I think about how much, it takes my breath away. So, when you see me gasping for air don't worry, I am only having an "I Love You" attack.

I Love You

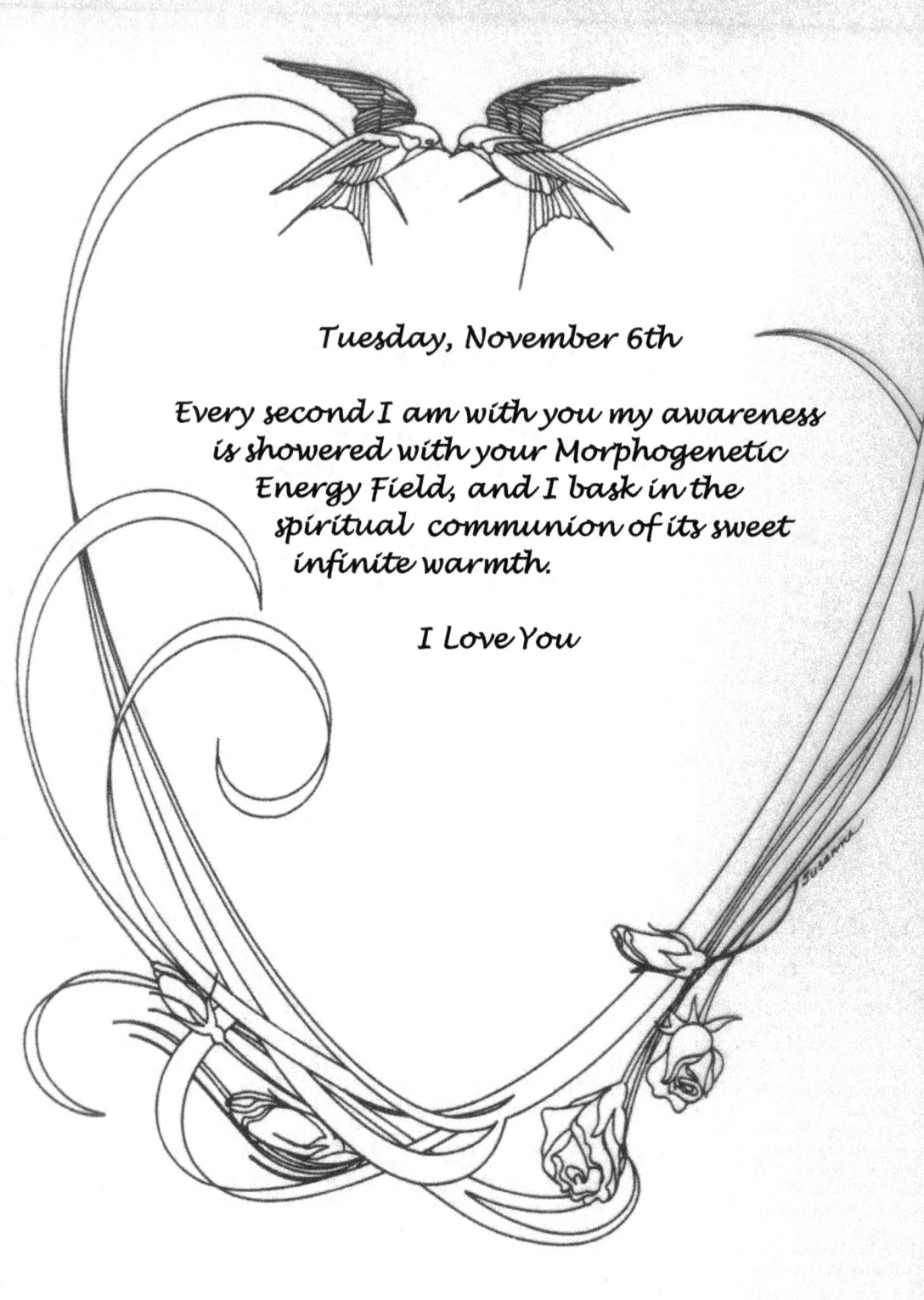

Tuesday, November 6th

Every second I am with you my awareness
is showered with your Morphogenetic
Energy Field, and I bask in the
spiritual communion of its sweet
infinite warmth.

I Love You

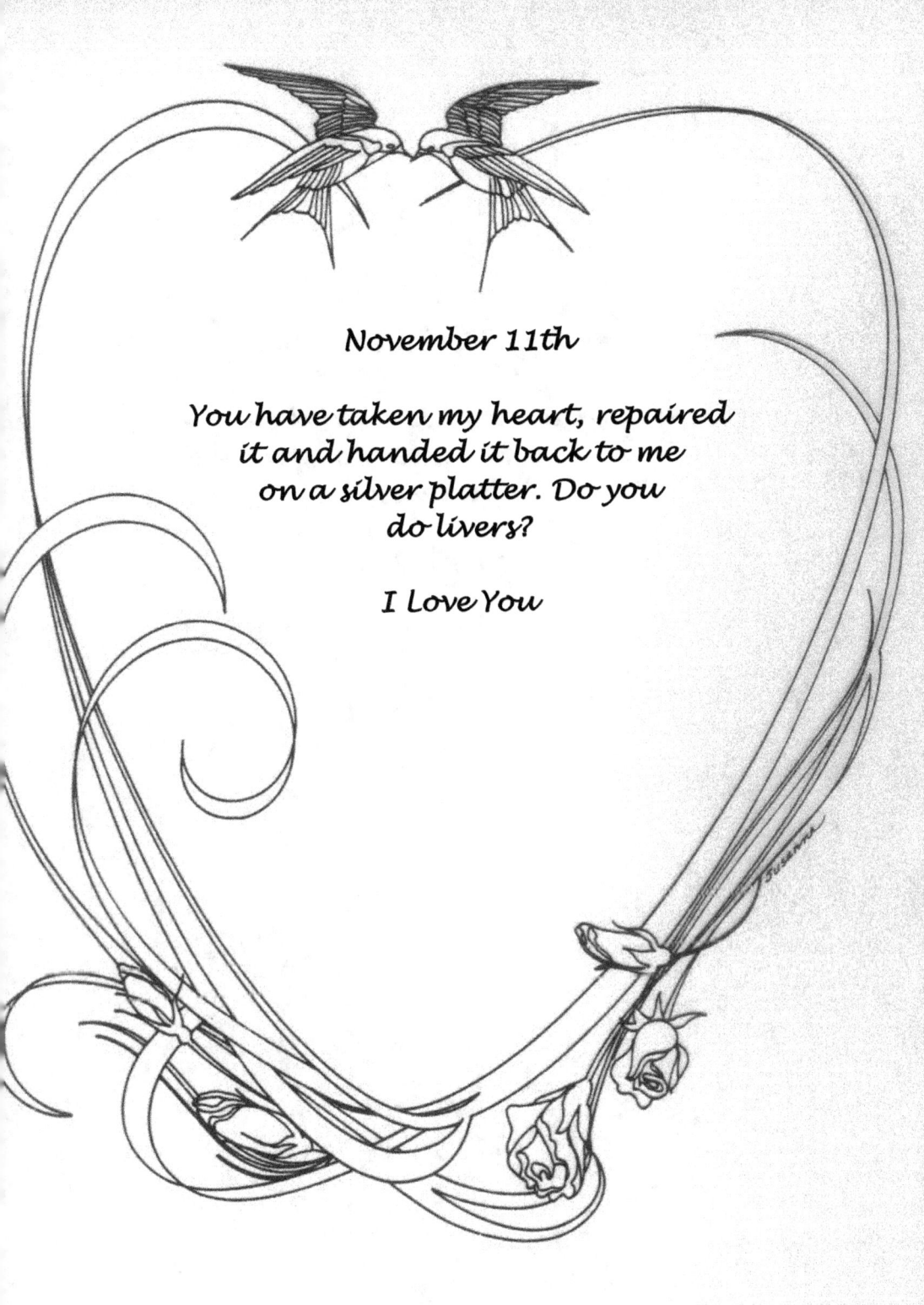

November 11th

*You have taken my heart, repaired
it and handed it back to me
on a silver platter. Do you
do livers?*

I Love You

Friday, November 14th

You are the most wonderful snuggle buddy in the history of snuggle buddies.

I Love You

Friday, November 21st

My tenure on this plane with you will be
an example to all who follow that
man's capacity to love can
reach incredible
dimensions.

I Love You

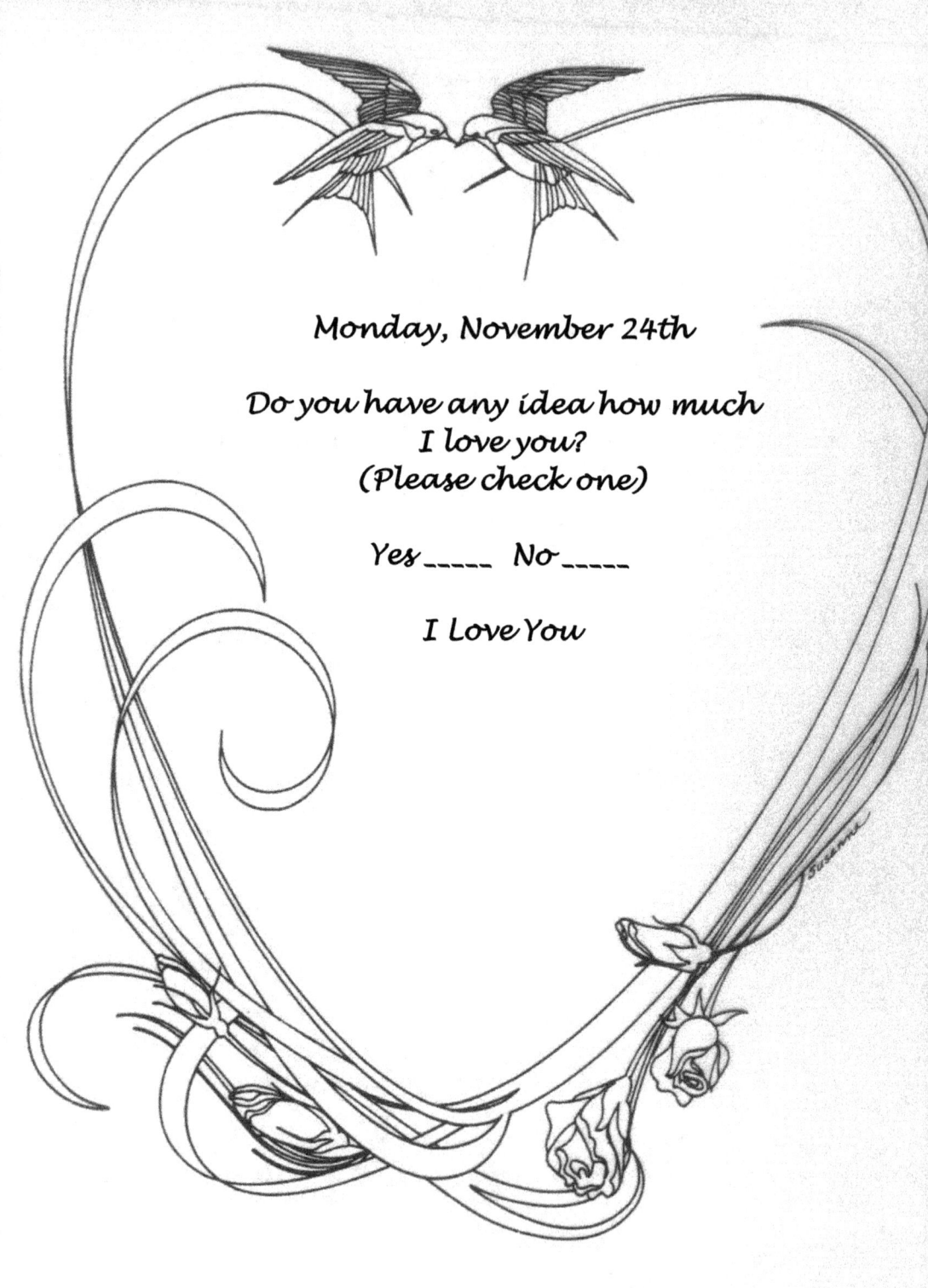

Monday, November 24th

Do you have any idea how much
I love you?
(Please check one)

Yes _____ No _____

I Love You

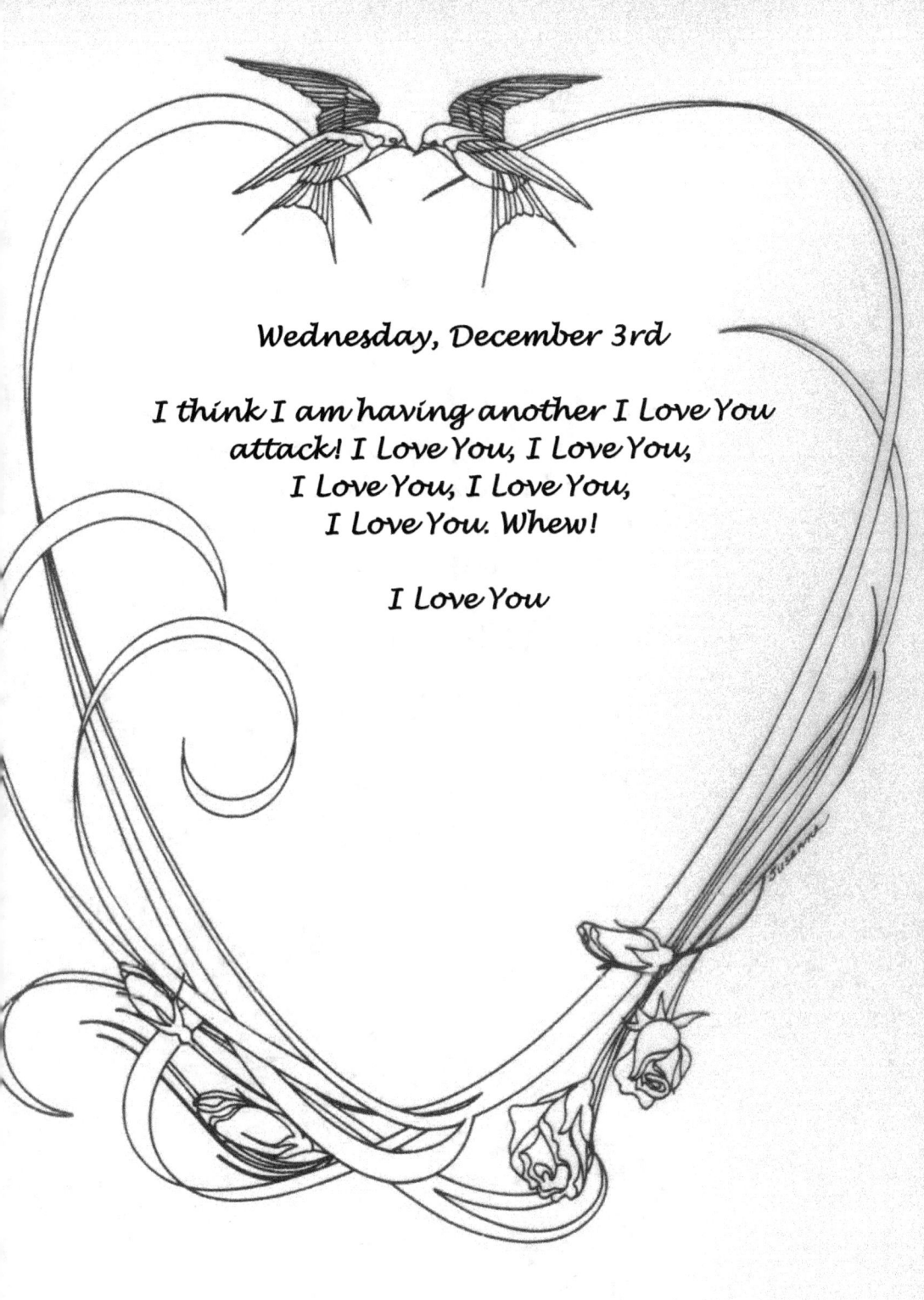

Wednesday, December 3rd

*I think I am having another I Love You
attack! I Love You, I Love You,
I Love You, I Love You,
I Love You. Whew!*

I Love You

Friday, December 19th

How frustrating it is to have experienced
infinity with you, and having only a
finite medium in which to communi-
cate it. Do you think maybe God
has a sense of humor?

I Love You

Tuesday, December 30th

Knowing that like attracts like and for me to have attracted you in my life, I must have been thinking the purest most beautiful thoughts ever to pass through anyone's mind.

I Love You

Tuesday, January 6th

Once upon a time before the Universe was created, God had just returned from vacation and wanted to get back into the swing of things. So, he decided to create a perfect female being. You were that creation. So pleased was he with his creation that he decided to create our Universe to give you a place to exist, (the bible scholars will really flip over this version) and that is why our Universe was created. Thank you for giving us all a place to live.

I Love You

Wednesday, January 14th

Before I met you I wasn't quite sure what love was. Now, I have so much of it I cannot find the words to adequately express it. It just goes to show you, if it isn't one thing, it's something else.

I Love You

Monday, February 24th

During my late night conversation
with you know who, he asked how we
were doing and I told him that liv-
ing with you was like living with
a Renoir, and that every day I
found something different to
appreciate about you. He
asked me to send his
regards to his most
favorite creation.
You!

I Love You

Wednesday, February 26th

Have I told you lately how very
much I love you? Just
checking.

I Love You

Friday, February 28th

Do you have any idea how fortunate I am to be your soul-mate? I wish I could show you how many people were inter viewed for the position. (Act-ually, I was the interviewer and when I saw who I was interviewing for I decid-ed to handle this one myself)

I Love You

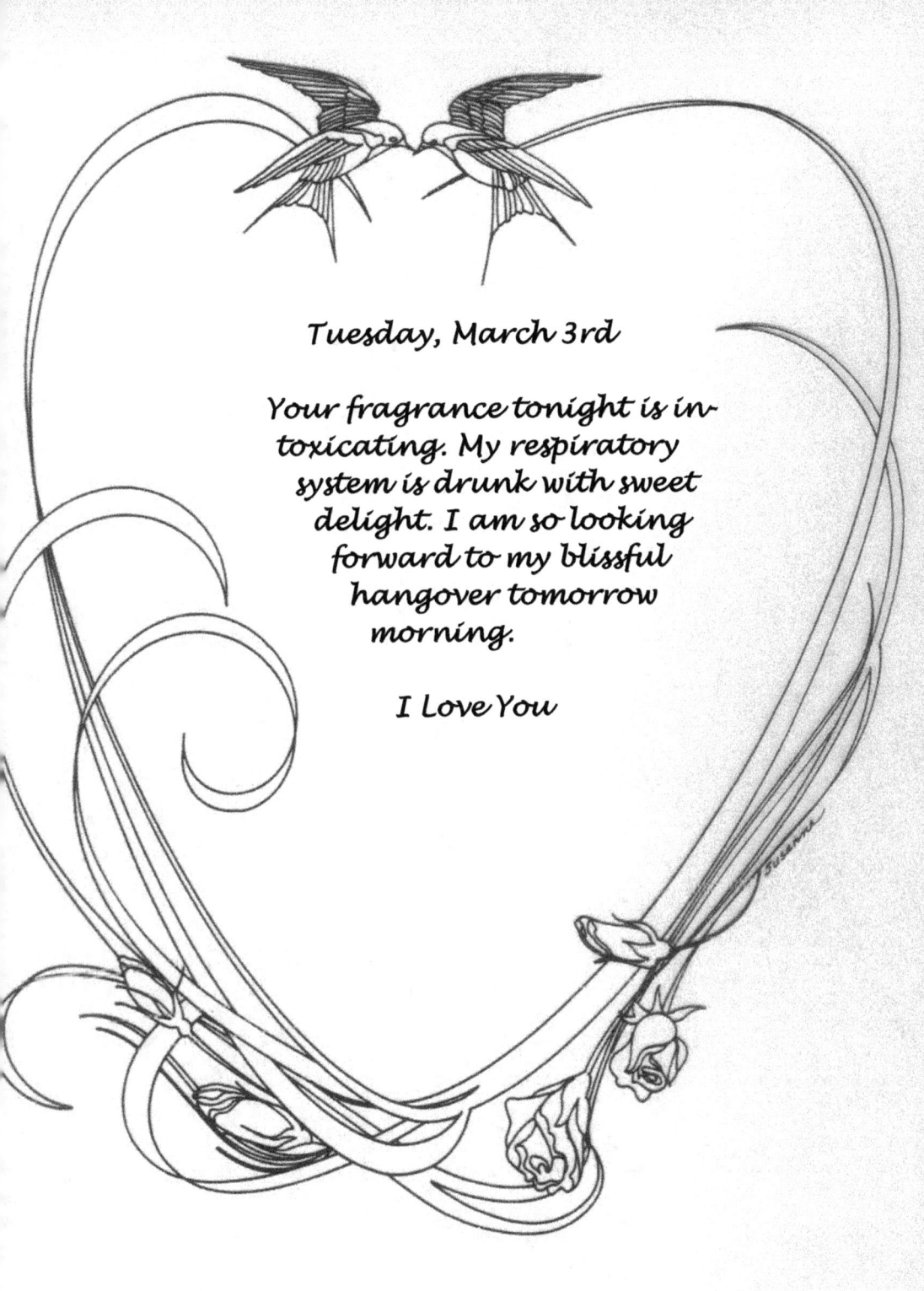

Tuesday, March 3rd

Your fragrance tonight is in-
toxicating. My respiratory
system is drunk with sweet
delight. I am so looking
forward to my blissful
hangover tomorrow
morning.

I Love You

Friday, March 5th

Will you ever cease to amaze
me? Gosh, I hope not.

I Love You

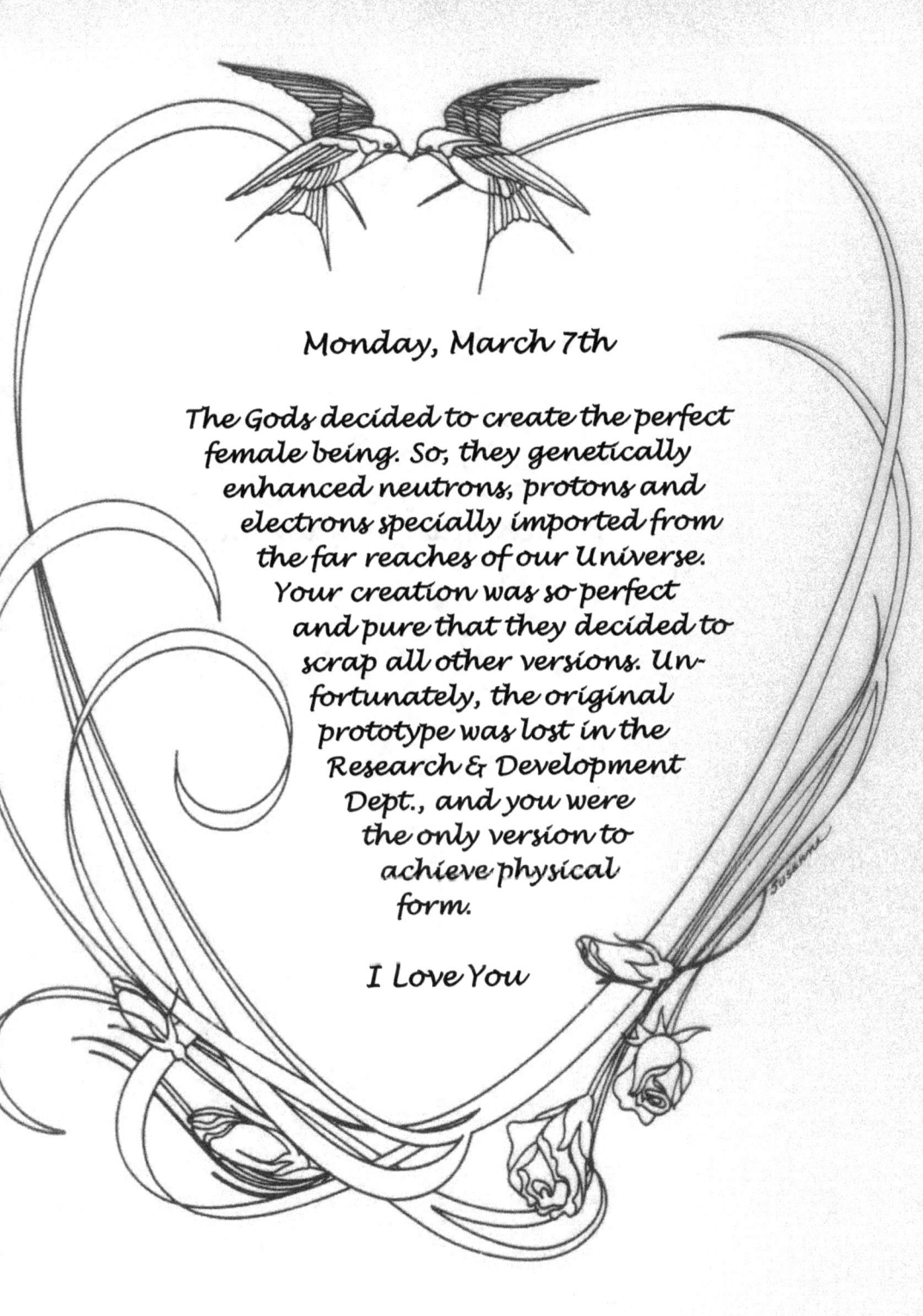

Monday, March 7th

The Gods decided to create the perfect
female being. So, they genetically
enhanced neutrons, protons and
electrons specially imported from
the far reaches of our Universe.
Your creation was so perfect
and pure that they decided to
scrap all other versions. Un-
fortunately, the original
prototype was lost in the
Research & Development
Dept., and you were
the only version to
achieve physical
form.

I Love You

Wednesday, March 9th

It delights me to no end to ob-
serve you,; doing nothing in
particular; just being your
enchantingly adorable
self.

I Love You

Friday, March 11th

Your voice is that of an angel
gently caressing my ears with
an infinite cacophony of the
sweetest sounds ever created
by vocal cords.

I Love You

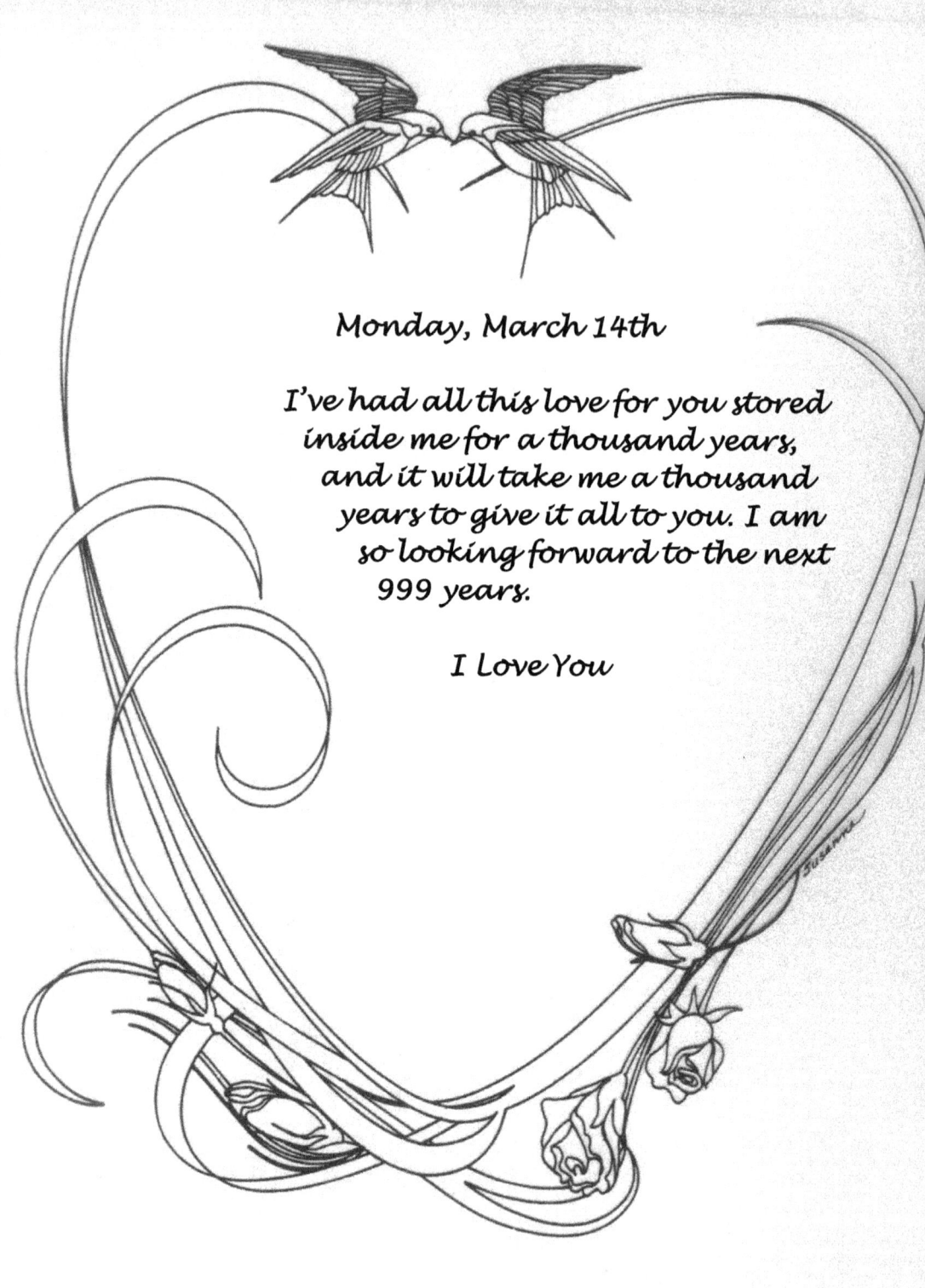

Monday, March 14th

I've had all this love for you stored inside me for a thousand years, and it will take me a thousand years to give it all to you. I am so looking forward to the next 999 years.

I Love You

Thursday, March 17th

On 2-12-48, I was given the option
of moving on to the next plane, or
moving through this one. I was
shown the years in advance.
Most were mundane. However,
when I reached the year 1984,
there was no doubt in my
mind where I belonged.
Thank you for being in
my future.

I Love You

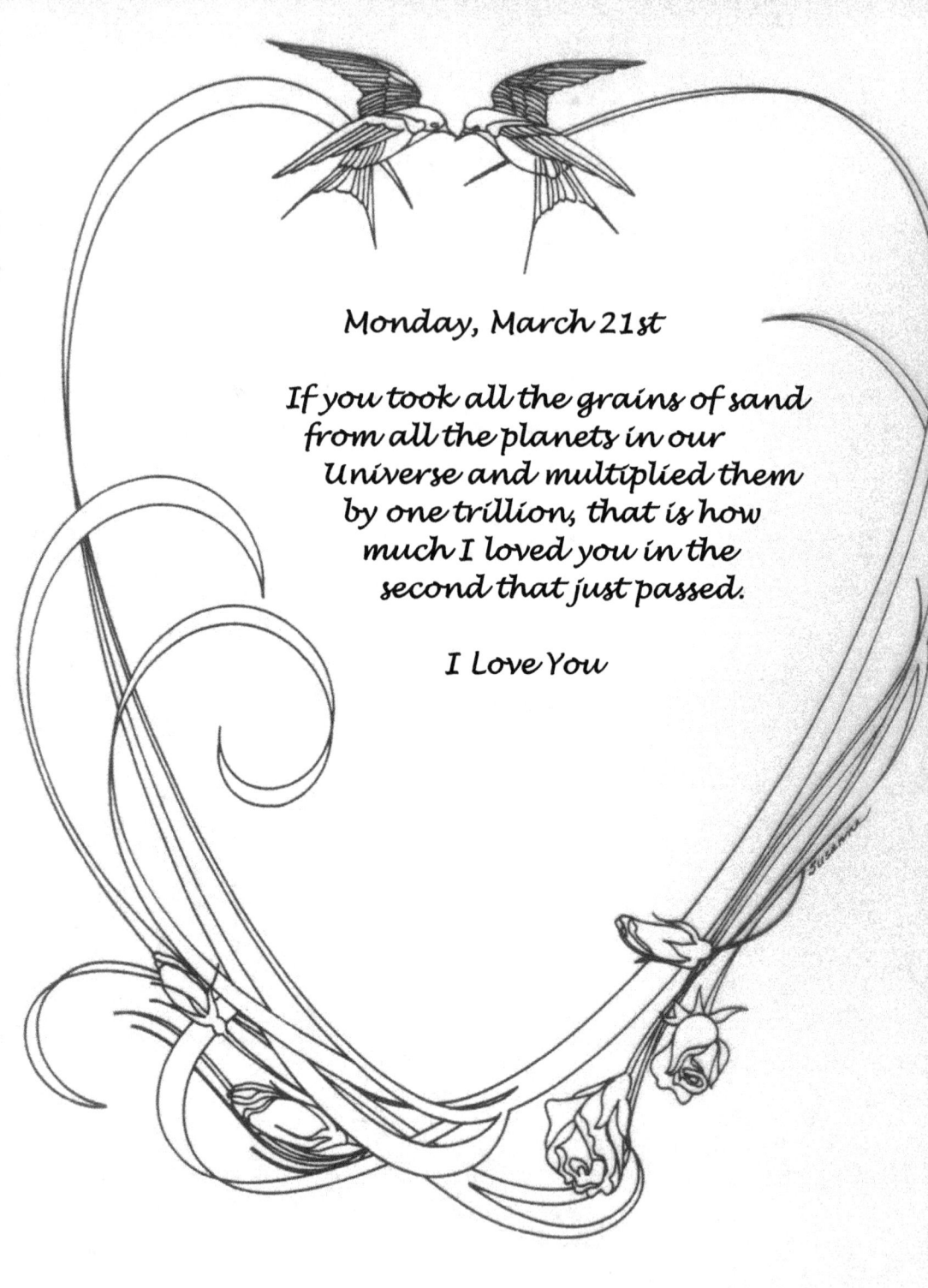

Monday, March 21st

If you took all the grains of sand
from all the planets in our
Universe and multiplied them
by one trillion, that is how
much I loved you in the
second that just passed.

I Love You

Wednesday, March 23rd

When we went to the beach yesterday I saw you walking towards the ocean in your white bikini. I thought, "My God! What a vision! I am the luckiest man to have ever achieved physical form on Planet Earth."

I Love You

Monday, March 28th

Before I met you I was very hard. Now I am very soft. That's because when I am in your presence every cell, organ and tissue in my body turns to silly putty.

I Love You

Wednesday, March 30th

I asked my heart how it felt
about you. Quite predictably,
it told me that life without
you is out of the question.
You see, my heart beats
only for you.

I Love You

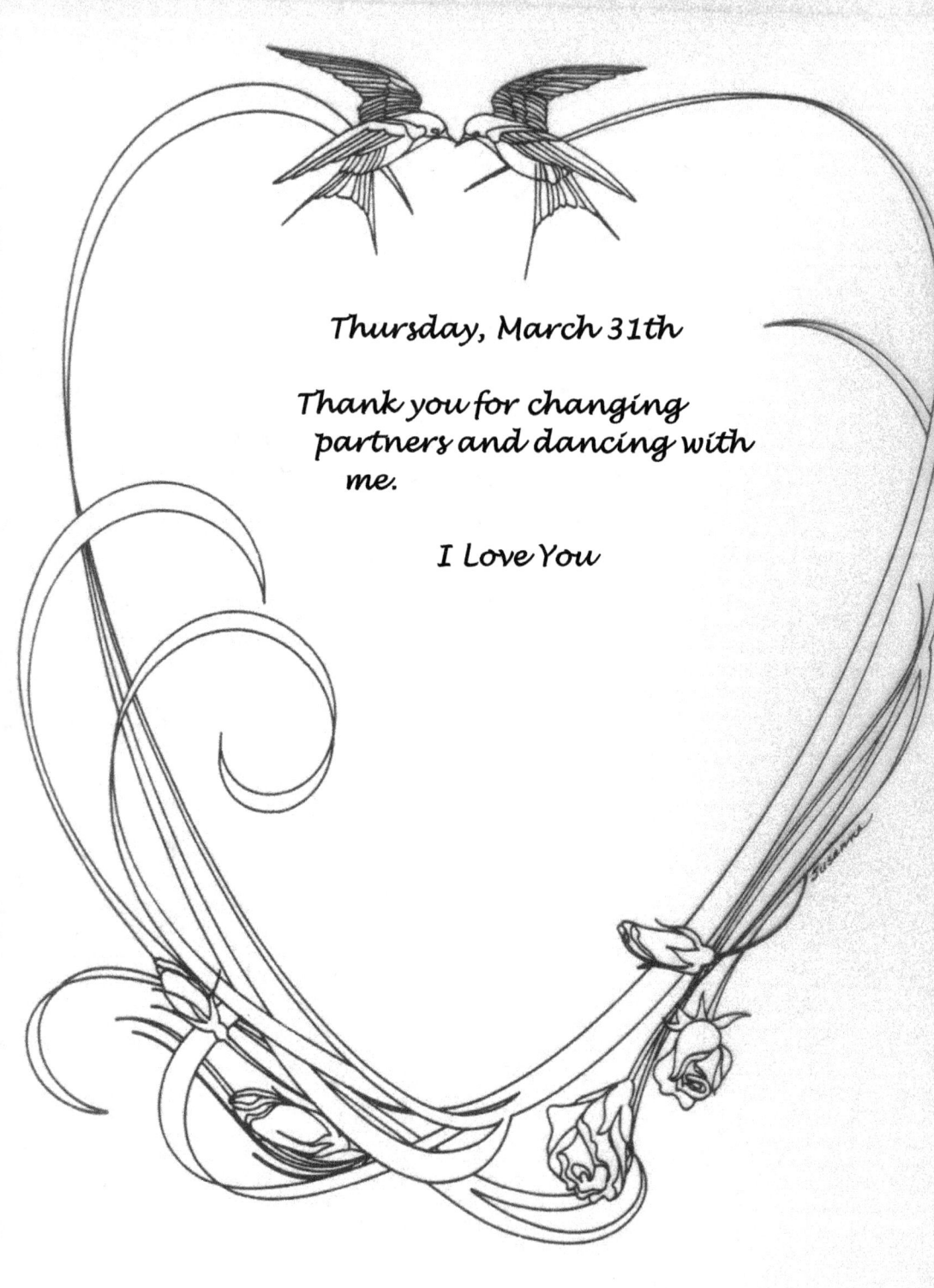

Thursday, March 31th

Thank you for changing
partners and dancing with
me.

I Love You

Tuesday, March 25th, 2014

In losing you, I feel like my
heart has been ripped out of
my chest, and that all joy
has been sucked out of my
life. Remember, if you get
scared when you get to
where you are going,
wait for me and I will
go with you. My baby,
I will love and
adore you forever.

I Love You

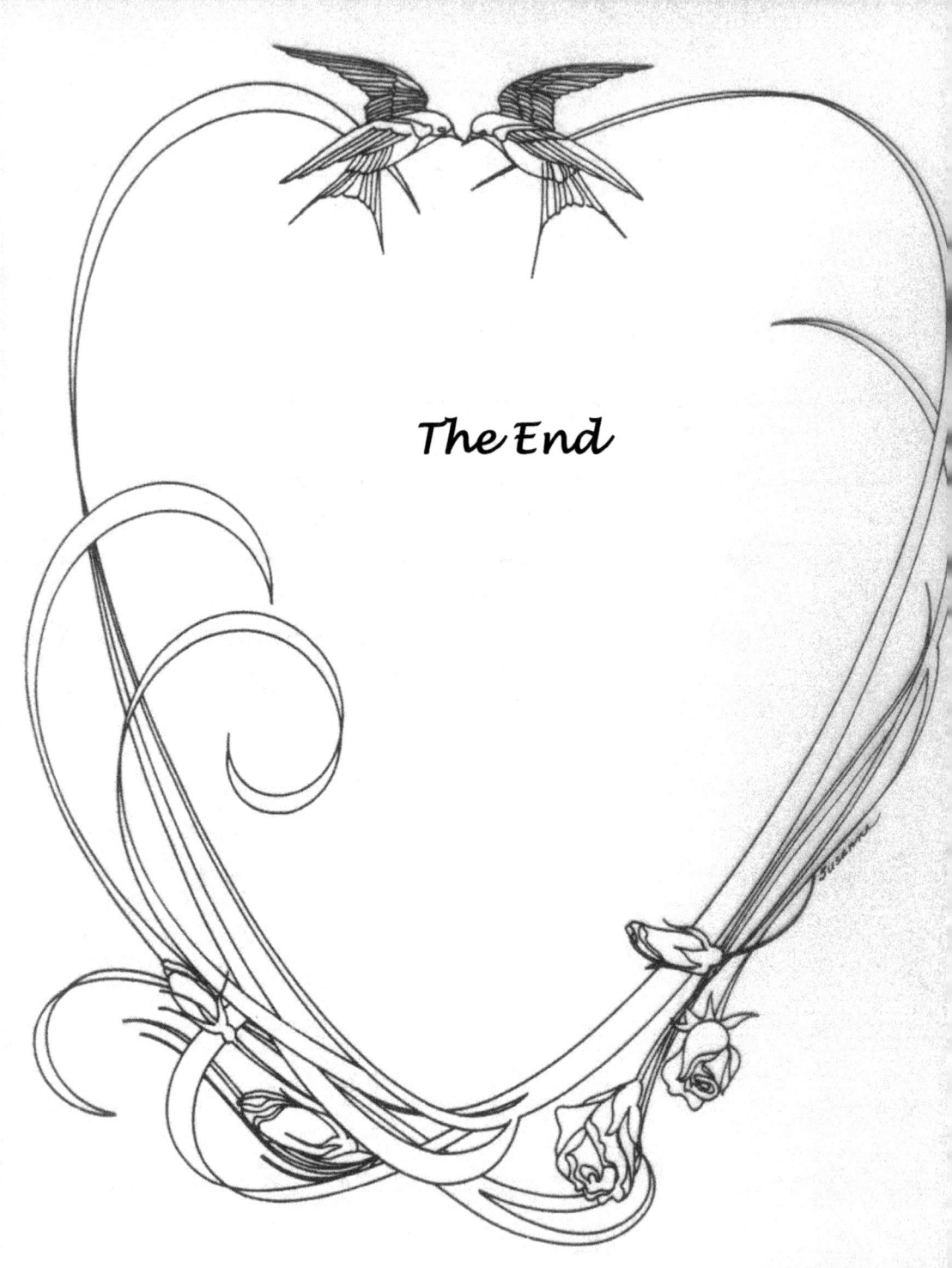

The End

www.ingramcontent.com/pod-product-compliance
Lightning Source LLC
Chambersburg PA
CBHW060128260626
47160CB00005B/2050